Clean Western Romance

BEACHES AND TRAILS
PUBLISHING

About the Author

Daisy Landish is a romance and cozy mystery author living in the UK, whose clean and sweet stories have tugged at readers' heartstrings across the pond and beyond. When she's not writing love stories, Daisy spends her time reading, hiking at dawn, and riding into the sunset on her horse, Rosebud.

Join Daisy's Newsletter for updates and giveaways!
www.daisylandishromance.com

facebook.com/daisylandishromance

x.com/daisy_landish

instagram.com/beachesandtrailspublishing

amazon.com/author/daisylandish

bookbub.com/authors/daisy-landish

goodreads.com/daisylandishromance

Also by Daisy Landish

Clean Regency Romance

The Lady Series - The Allington Collection

The Lady Series - The Gillingham Collection

The Lady Series - The Blackmore Collection

The Lady Series - The Norrington Collection

Clean Contemporary Romance

Love on Spruce Island

Second Chance

Cherry Tree Island

The Wedding Trio

Extra Credit

Counting on the Cowboy

Focusing on the Cowboy

Mistletoe Magic

Cozy Mysteries

Jane and Kennedy Daniels Mysteries

Pine Grove Mysteries

Annie Archer Paranormal Mysteries

Wilma Wade Holiday Mysteries

Mike and Maddie Mysteries

Mystic Moonhaven Mysteries

Sweater Weather: Cozy Mysteries for Fall

Summer Vibes: Cozy Mysteries for Summer

One

⁓

AT FIRST, Camilla Santos wasn't quite sure why she was more excited about this photography assignment than she'd been about any of her others. This was likely to be the most laid-back freelance project she'd ever had by all accounts, and by any stretch of her imagination. She concluded that must be it as she dodged her way through the large crowd at Denver International Airport. This time she'd have a chance to relax while working, and she'd also have time to enjoy herself. Photographing war zones and significant sporting events had been exciting, earning her accolades across the globe. But this new assignment to document life in the Great Plains carried a more engaging, different, and larger challenge. This time around, the setting and activities within themselves weren't thrilling; she'd have to capture people, places, and events in such a way as to bring out their magic for people to see.

Right now, though, she just wanted to get out of the busy airport, and she scanned the signs above to find her baggage claim. Spotting it far off in the distance, she sighed and continued navigating her way through the people who were rushing to get somewhere else. This was the problem in large cities, she decided. Everyone was always in a hurry, in a mad rush to get somewhere, thinking only of themselves. Not that she expected any of the strangers to slow down or stop long enough to have a friendly chat with her. It was just very apparent that city people were so entrenched in their own lives that they rarely even noticed anything or anyone else. Suddenly remembering she'd forgotten to call Ann when she landed, she pulled her cell from her pocket while juggling her camera bag that served as her purse and carry-on.

Sliding sideways at the last moment, she narrowly avoided a wayward toddler squealing and obliviously running straight toward her. The kid would have smacked straight into her if she hadn't seen her in time. The little girl's mother scurried behind her, grabbing her daughter's arm while smiling apologetically.

"So sorry," she mumbled. "She's such a handful and doesn't travel well!"

"No problem at all," Camilla returned her smile. "I totally get it. I'm an aunt."

Camilla called after her as the frazzled mom turned and began walking away with her now pouting child. The little girl was adorable, dressed like a mini cowgirl, with a cowboy hat and tiny leather boots. Camilla thought them to be the perfect subject for her first photos as she explained who she was and her assignment to the mother, who was relieved her daughter hadn't created too much of a stir.

"Smile for the camera, Jenny. Show this nice woman what a great cowgirl you already are!"

Jenny laughed and giggled as she posed, even asking her mother if she had a lasso for her to throw. Laughing, her mom explained to Camilla that she had a small replica lasso she tossed through the air while riding her rocking horse.

"That would have been a fantastic picture," Camilla told her as she redirected Jenny's pose.

After a few more clicks of her camera, she thanked them before placing it back in her bag and wandering off. Hopefully, the rest of my assignment will be just as easy and run as smoothly, she thought as she grabbed her phone again. Nothing over the top exciting to report yet, but she'd promised to call her best friend as soon as she landed. Ann answered mid-way through the second ring.

"Two questions. Did you meet a hot and rich rancher yet, and does he have a brother?"

Camilla burst out laughing.

"Whoa there, girlfriend. Your second question assumes I said yes to the first. I'm afraid there is no rich, hot rancher yet, but I just took some shots of a sweet little cowgirl."

She explained how the toddler had been running away from her mother and how she'd nearly come crashing into her.

"Well, keep your gaze far above your kneecaps," Ann joked, "and eyes peeled for those rugged, handsome cowboys reeking of thousand-dollar bills."

Laughing hard as she dodged three sprinting businessmen who weren't paying attention, Camilla ran straight into a huge metal trash can.

"Great..." she mumbled, leaving Ann wondering what the noise was, sidestepping quickly to the right, only to run right into a stern-looking man who definitely wasn't amused. "Shit. Sorry," she murmured again, barely suppressing her laughter as the man shook his head and stormed off.

"Hey, what's happening there? Sounds like you're back in another war zone," Ann giggled.

"Nope. Just lovely Denver International. The only landmines here are people in such a hurry that they're not paying attention to where they're going. I'll be so glad to get to Cheyenne, Wyoming, with less people and more personal space."

She quickly gave Ann the details of where she would be staying in Cheyenne, how long she'd be there photographing the town's Frontier Days festivities, the quiet country roads, fields of crops, and whatever else she could find and that best represented the Great Plains.

"Make sure to call the authorities," she added, "if you haven't heard from me in a few days, let them know I'm starving, dehydrated, and lost in the wilderness."

"Well, Miss Photojournalist," Ann laughed, "guess you didn't do your preliminary research so well this time around. I can tell you without a doubt that, as a native of western Nebraska, I passed through Wyoming dozens of times and there's nothing even remotely close to wilderness where you'll be. It's just prairie land. You're more likely to be bitten by a snake or chased by a buffalo."

"Wonderful. You know how I practically faint at the sight of snakes," Camilla snickered, dodging to her left to narrowly avoid a carelessly pushed baggage cart with a family's luggage tossed on so haphazardly it threatened to fly off.

Thankfully, she eventually made it to her designated baggage area in one piece. Now all she had to do was make it out of this part of the maze alive long enough to get to the other end of the airport to pick up her reserved rental car. She told Ann before signing off and promising to call her once she'd checked into her hotel in Cheyenne; it shouldn't be too difficult. Inching her way through the crowd to the front of the luggage carousel, she sensed she had a long wait. It rotated empty with not a single suitcase in sight. She tried to make small talk, but no one around her seemed especially interested. It had been a long flight, and everyone was antsy to get on their way. Searching for more photo subjects, she spotted two cowboys she hadn't noticed on the plane. Might as well grab some pics of them too, she thought. They did fit the western stereotype, and anything was better than just standing there.

"Excuse me," she tapped the arm of one of them after she'd gently shoved her way through the crowd. "I'm Camilla Santos, and I'm a photojournalist on assignment for Geographic Insight Magazine. I'm documenting the Great Plains. Do you mind if I take a few photos of you guys?"

She unzipped her camera bag quickly, pulling out two of her business cards. The men took them, surprised. The tallest one smirked.

"Why would you want pictures of us? We're just two regular guys returning from a business trip."

"You look like cowboys; I mean because of your hats. I'm just trying to get a sense of what people are like everywhere I go on this trip."

"Where else you headed but Denver?" the other guy asked.

Camilla elaborated upon her upcoming two-and-a-half-hour drive to Cheyenne and her planned activities there.

"Well, sure," he said, nodding to his companion. "Jake, let's let her get some shots."

The first photos she took were somewhat awkward. The men had no idea what to do, how to stand, or what expression to have on their faces. These reactions were nothing new to her, so Camilla did her best to joke around and help them to relax. Within a few minutes, she had them posing, smiling at the camera, looking off intently into the distance, and even shaking hands as though they'd just gotten together or recently met.

"Thanks so much, guys!" she smiled before walking away.

She loved it when people were cooperative and when they ended up enjoying the quick photoshoot as much as she did herself. Seeing no one else she longed to capture on camera, she went back to the carousel. It finally had a few suitcases on it, so at least she was one step closer to getting on her way. Her own bags seemed to take forever, and she lost herself in thought until they arrived. As much as she loved her freelance photography career, she was slowly getting to the point where she wanted to travel a little less and maybe start thinking about more than her job. At thirty-five years old, she'd be the last of her sisters to get married, if, in fact, she ever got married at all.

Boyfriends had never been her main priority. Even back in her teens while all her friends fell in and out of love every few months. For as long as she could remember, the camera had been her most favored companion, at her side always since grade school. Sure, she'd dated lots of guys growing up, and even had two serious relationships more recently. But her love for photography and adventure had always taken precedence. Slowly but surely, each of her romantic relationships had fizzled out as a result. *Maybe Ann's right*, she mused. *I better start looking for a rich, remarkably handsome cowboy while I'm here.* She realized she was smiling widely and quickly neutralized her expression before anyone around her noticed as she grabbed the first of her bags.

The rental car areas were no less busy. She groaned upon arriving there. She resolved herself to a long wait as she ambled up to the line to stand behind a young girl in cowboy boots with a particularly short blue jean mini skirt.

"How fast is this line moving?" she asked her, eager to finally get out of the airport and be on her way.

"Not fast," the young blonde laughed. "I've been here for about ten minutes, and it hasn't budged."

"Great..."

"You're not from here, are you?" the girl asked her.

She looked to be in her late teens.

"Is it that obvious?" Camilla laughed. "No, I'm from Connecticut. I mean, originally. Now I live in Maryland."

With nothing else to do, they enjoyed some easy conversation. It turned out that the teenager, Lilah, had recently been declared first runner-up for the title of Miss Texas, and the pageant's talent competition had helped launch her country music career as a singer. She was in Denver to attend her cousin's wedding and now she was off to Nashville to meet with an agent very interested in managing her and securing a record deal.

"Wow, congratulations! That's so exciting," Camilla gushed, remembering her enthusiasm for her own career during her teens. "Hey, since you're from Texas, maybe I could include you in my photojournalism project on the Great Plains."

No sooner than she'd explained her assignment, Lilah pulled out a hand mirror from her purse and quickly began reapplying her lipstick and fixing her hair. Right away, as she began posing, even for the casual-looking shots, it was apparent that she was no stranger to the camera. She told Camilla that she'd spent much of her childhood modeling and competing in pageants from the time she was four. Not exactly a rancher or a buffalo, Camilla smiled to herself later, but certainly, a great depiction of Great Plains style American Pie. She was finally at the car rental counter, casually daydreaming about what it would have been like to enter beauty pageants when she'd been younger when the agent startled her out of her reverie by handing her the keys.

"Out through those doors," she pointed, "and to the parking lot to your left. Your car's color and license plate number are on the top right of your rental agreement. Any questions or concerns at all, just call our toll-free number for help."

Surprising herself, she was still daydreaming about beauty pageants as she pulled out of the maze of traffic clogging just about every area of the airport. Lilah had mentioned she had a boyfriend, not a new guy she'd met since winning her title, but one who'd started out as her best friend from the time she was twelve. Humph, she grunted. I wouldn't have been likely to win any beauty pageants but maybe I'd have a long-time boyfriend too if I'd spent more time cultivating all sorts of friendships instead of concentrating solely on my photography. Glancing quickly into the rear-view mirror before pulling off the exit ramp and merging into highway traffic, she continued pondering her life situation. Although not beauty contestant material, she certainly was very attractive with her long dark brown hair, styled in waves, and her dark brown eyes. A fitness buff, she turned heads wherever she went. Maybe Ann's right, she mused. I ought to start paying attention to which men are paying attention to me.

For now, at least, her attention turned to Colorado. As she drove, she marveled at how beautiful it was. The further she got from the airport and outer city, the more mesmerizing it all became. The spectacular Rocky Mountains towered in the distance, and she pulled off the highway at rest stops more than once to zoom in and take some great shots. Although she'd taken pictures of the Himalayas, and other spectacular mountain ranges during her travels, there was something awe-inspiring about mountains found within your own country and home. That's the thing about America, she thought as she got back in her car. Even though not everyone travels from state to state, we're more patriotic and appreciative of our country than most.

Construction sites dotted the landscape before she completely left the suburbs behind. Somehow out of place as the miles of farm fields loomed in the distance, she quickly pulled over and got photos of the partially-erect buildings too. They signified commerce and economic development, as well as a rising population amid natural beauty and pristine habitat. As she was taking pictures of the miles of farm fields from her vantage point at a rest stop much further along in her trip, a huge truck pulled in and parked in the corner. She watched a suntanned middle-aged female trucker climb out of the cab.

"Tourist?" the smiling woman asked her as she ambled up.

"Kind of. I'm looking at things from that point of view."

She quickly explained her assignment and decided to ask the trucker if she could take photos of her too.

"Me?" the woman laughed. "You can't possibly think I'm worthy of a cover shot or even a spot in the magazine."

Camilla laughed at her very normal response. Almost everyone she'd ever taken photos of, except for athletes and celebrities, felt this same way. She clarified she was shooting the reality of the Great Plains. Real landscape, real people that were a part of it. It took a little bit of convincing but the trucker, who told her that her name was Hannah, finally agreed. Camilla got some great candid shots of her by the barricade at the far end of the rest stop, gazing off into the distance at the fields of sweet corn that stretched for miles. After that, she took pictures of her standing in front of her truck and then when she was seated back in the cab. Surprisingly, as soon as Camilla was done, Hannah quickly scrambled back out.

"No worries," she told her, noticing the bewildered look on her face. "I stopped to walk around and stretch my legs for a bit, and I haven't done that yet."

"Oh, so sorry," Camilla apologized. "Sometimes I get so wrapped up in my photos, especially when I manage to include random people, that I forget that I'm interrupting their lives."

"I get like that when I'm driving," Hannah confided in her, "especially on long hauls. I get so focused on reaching my destination that I get annoyed by people slowing me down, veering in and out of traffic all around me, forgetting that they're focused on goals of their own, getting to work, maybe to appointments, or just to get home."

They chatted for a few minutes about the challenges and demands of their careers. Camilla was putting her camera away when her stomach growled loud enough for Hannah to hear.

"Now that's another problem," her new acquaintance smirked, "finding good places to eat when on the road."

Grabbing her cell and googling the nearest restaurants, Camilla found a list of them in Keenesburg. Deno's was one of the closest and dominated the internet with fantastic reviews. Scrolling the menu as Hannah looked over her shoulder, Camilla was pleasantly surprised at Hannah's first-hand knowledge of the local food scene. She'd eaten at Deno's numerous times, and recommended it highly.

"It's a great spot, and the people are friendly. You won't be disappointed if you give it a try."

After thanking her for her advice, Camilla was soon on the road again. She still had a way to go before leaving Colorado and reaching Wyoming, so there was no sense in waiting to get something to eat.

Too bad Ann isn't with me, she mused, as she remembered the great times they'd had hanging out together. Just me today, Camilla smirked. You'll just have to enjoy your own company and amuse yourself for once.

Two

~~~

NOT EVEN TEN MINUTES LATER, Camilla was pulling off the highway onto the exit ramp and then slowing down to enter Keenesburg, one of the tiniest American towns she'd ever been in. Population 1,312, the welcome sign informed her. Wow. Her high school, and most certainly her college, had way more people than that. Probably the neighborhood where she lived in Baltimore, Maryland had many more than that too. Suddenly, she longed to remain. If not exactly forever in Keenesburg, then at least somewhere in the Great Plains. Less hustle and bustle, smiling, happy people everywhere, she mused, as she drove the two blocks to Deno's. The diner wasn't hard to find at all. Its large red and white sign was pretty much the first thing anyone noticed when they pulled into town. Full parking lot, she grinned as she took the second last spot. Although surprised the tiny restaurant was so busy, she took it as a great sign of good food.

Almost leaving her camera bag on the passenger seat, she decided to take it with her as she slid out of the car. Three laughing children raced by her in the parking lot, followed more slowly by their chatting parents, who were also headed for the front door. With about as many people entering as there were leaving, Deno's looked to be the place to go for miles around. As the savory smells of delicious food wafted toward her on the gentle breeze, Camilla decided to capture the downhome scenery of this place as well. Pulling her camera out from her bag, she marveled at how much the diner looked like something out of a Norman Rockwell painting. And not on purpose, she grinned, simply because that's what it was. After snapping a few photos from various angles and locations in the parking lot, she succumbed to her ever-grumbling stomach and hurried inside.

Standing room only; she wasn't all that perturbed. She glanced at the huge round clock on the wall. It was getting to the end of what could be considered lunch hour, and the place was still packed. I'm in no rush really, she pondered. Besides, every place she visited on her trip offered opportunities for extra pictures. She'd learned from many years of experience that it was always better to have way more shots to choose from than she'd ever utilize in the end. At a standstill in the lineup and milling crowd, she glanced around for more prospective photo subjects. Patrons looked to be either truckers or locals, and maybe a traveling tourist or two.

"If you don't have your sights set on a table, there's space at the counter," a harried waitress announced as she scurried by carrying a huge tray full of heaping platefuls of food and drinks.

When no one moved, Camilla decided to jump on the opportunity for a quicker meal herself. Squeezing through the smiling and laughing crowd as best she could without bashing anyone with her large and heavy camera bag, she found that she wasn't all that successful at avoiding this form of assault. She'd no sooner smashed her bag against an elderly woman's hip, apologizing profusely, then she rammed it into a teenager's stomach when she turned.

"I'm so sorry," she felt her face flush, as she slowly inched her way through the crowd.

I should be better at navigating my camera through tight spaces by now, she chided herself just as she bumped into a short, incredibly overweight trucker. She was forced to apologize again and again. When someone bumped into her for a change, she quickly stepped back, only to bang her camera bag against someone else. She spun to apologize but paused for a second. This guy was different, more handsome and rugged than any of the others she'd seen on this trip. A cowboy, for sure. A real cowboy and not an imitation dressed that way as a cultural or fashion statement and to impress. His light green eyes bored into hers as she stared at him in awe for a moment before saying anything. Tall, muscular, tanned, she checked off his attributes silently in her mind. Stoic. The kind of cowboy starring in old westerns. The kind of guy that made his female co-star sigh and swoon into his strong arms at the end of the film.

"Wow, so sorry about that," she finally blurted. "It's just so crowded in here."

He said nothing, nodding politely before disappearing into the jostling crowd. Just wonderful, Camilla groaned. First, assault the man of your dreams, then blame it on the crowd around you. Nothing like making yourself look like an inept fool, unable to safely handle your own equipment. Not that he likely even noticed I'm a photographer anyway, she sulked as she made her way to the counter as quickly as she could. And not like he looked like the type of guy that her job would impress in the least. She'd only made contact for a second but somehow sensed that he was far too down to earth for that and much too grounded to be impressed by exotic tales of her travels and harrowing photographic feats. No sooner had she plunked herself onto a tall stool at the counter when the flustered waitress reappeared.

"What'll you have?" she snipped.

"Oh!" Shocked, Camilla noticed the laminated menu on the counter in front of her. "Sorry, I just sat down and need a few minutes to decide."

The waitress huffed and walked away. So much for downhome hospitality as far as she's concerned, Camilla snickered as she pulled the menu closer. She's one person I definitely don't want photos of, she thought as she scanned the offerings of food and drinks. Great. All the dishes had wonderful, cowboy-esque-sounding names with no explanations of what they were, aside from the menu's section titles which were just as vague. Roundup, Good & Hearty, Lasso Lovers, For Wranglers, Just for Champions. Yeah, right. Taking a closer read, she surmised that everything under the Roundup section was basically some sort of appetizer or starter dish. But that's as much as she figured out. What the hell were Rancher Twists? Glancing around, she saw that no one else already eating or with a menu in front of them looked

12

perplexed. Regulars, she realized, or the odd tourist who'd been wise enough to ask.

"Ready?" the waitress startled her.

She had no less of an unwelcoming expression on her face.

"Afraid not," Camilla smirked and held her ground. "I can't tell what anything is on this menu. Would you be kind enough to explain it quickly so I can make a choice?"

"If you haven't noticed, it's super busy in here right now. You want an explanation for everything on the entire menu?! How about you just narrow it down for me a little, and we'll go from there. You in the mood for a quick snack, soup, sandwich, a burger, some kind of pasta, steak, ham, breakfast or dessert?"

She talked so fast that Camilla wasn't even sure she'd caught it all. The only thing she was sure of was that she was incredibly hungry and not about to make a choice without learning more about the available selection. She glared back at her. Dammit, I'm the paying customer, she thought. Not an annoyance or inconvenience. She leaned forward.

"No idea until you tell me what's actually on the menu," she smirked.

"Look..." the server's face heated, "We got six kinds of burgers alone. If you really..."

"Such as?" Camilla quipped, "With bacon and cheese? Cheese and mushroom? What? Just a quick description of stuff and..."

"Woah, there," a deep voice behind Camilla startled them both. "Hi, Sally. How you doing today? Busier in here than inside a beehive. I'm sure you've been running yourself ragged. Why don't I do you a little favor and help this lady out. I've eaten here so much I know this menu like the back of my hand."

Camilla turned and gasped. It was the cowboy, and he had a huge smile on his face.

"Sure, Beau. I'd be grateful," the waitress smiled for the first time since Camilla had entered the diner. "I'll come back and take the order in a little bit."

Just then, the old man in overalls on the stool to Camilla's right pushed his empty plate away, stood, and left. Beau eased onto the seat. Leaning closer to Camilla as he grabbed the menu, he slid it toward them. She couldn't help but notice the calluses on his strong, weathered hands. A true, hardworking cowboy who lived off the land. He removed his cowboy hat, setting it on the counter, and began to explain the maze of offerings available for her to eat.

"OK, right here under Roundup, you have your appetizers. Rancher Twists are breaded, deep-fried cheese. They're excellent, by the way; I've had them plenty of times myself," he nodded and smiled.

As he pointed at everything on the menu while translating it into its common name, Camilla realized she was having trouble concentrating on anything but the smooth, comforting sound of his rugged, even voice. What the hell's wrong with me, she wondered, as she struggled to maintain her focus. But she already knew. Beau was different from any of the men she'd met in her life. Confident yet unassuming, and gallantly polite. Nothing like the overly-attentive, eager to please, and even more eager to bed type of dudes she'd run across up until now.

"Make more sense?" he asked, looking at her squarely, raising his eyebrow in a maddeningly seductive-without-trying-to-be way.

"Yup," she smiled, secretly amused that she'd missed more than half of what he'd said. "Thanks so much. I really appreciate it."

He leaned closer, speaking quietly because the waitress loomed nearby.

"I hate rude people, and you looked lost."

Stunned for a moment, Camilla couldn't answer. He'd thought the waitress was rude? Well, she had been incredibly rude without question, but that wasn't the point. He'd spoken to her so politely, as if she was an old friend, offering to do her a favor by helping her customer out. This guy's a true gentleman to the core, she marveled. And, of course, I have to meet him sixteen hundred miles from home while briefly passing through his area on a business trip no less.

"Is she always so...abrupt?" she asked.

"Pretty much," Beau laughed. "But I like to give people the benefit of the doubt. No telling what's going on in her life besides this demanding job that keeps her hopping through her entire shift."

"Yeah," Camilla nodded, amazed that old western charm still existed in this crazy world.

"If you're in the mood for steak at all," he said, changing the subject,

"I highly recommend the Top Sirloin. You won't find a better steak dinner anywhere."

"Oh, really? It's good then? You've had it here before?"

"Plenty of times. I got to admit, I'm a fantastic cook but I couldn't make it better myself."

"Hmmm," Camilla nodded, silently thinking he's great-looking and he cooks too. "I like cooking myself, but I have to admit steak isn't my strong point. I mean," she stammered, embarrassed for a moment, "I don't absolutely demolish it, but I can't say it's my specialty."

"What is your specialty?" he grinned.

"Don't laugh."

"I won't," he promised, already laughing but crossing his heart in a chivalrous gesture.

She laughed too.

"It's meatloaf. I really excel at comfort food."

"Comfort food's important," he joked. "Without it we'd all be a mess sometimes."

"Well, I doubt it actually solves problems, but at least it makes people feel good," she smiled.

They'd been chatting casually for a few minutes when Sally returned to take her order. She asked for the Top Sirloin, smiling at Beau. Looking perplexed for a second, Sally shook her head and simply asked what she wanted to drink. She returned with the large glass of chocolate milk right away.

"Don't know that I've ever had a craving for chocolate milk with steak," Beau gazed at her, amused. "But maybe it's part of that comfort food thing."

"I guess so," she snickered, pondering how easy and relaxing it was to chat with this guy. Wishing, in a strange kind of way, that their conversation would never end.

"Here you go," Sally had returned and leaned over the counter, handing Beau a large paper bag filled with food.

"Takeout?" Camilla questioned, disappointed.

She'd been about to ask him to join her for lunch.

"Yup. It's Top Sirloin too," he grinned.

They looked at each other awkwardly for a moment before saying their goodbyes.

"Nice meeting you," Beau tipped his hat before turning to walk away.

"Wait!" Camilla spun on her stool.

Damn, she chided herself. Can I sound any more desperate? He stopped in his tracks and looked curiously at her.

"I mean, I'd love to take a few photos of you before you go."

"Photos? What for? I don't think so," he shook his head.

He was looking at her like she was crazy. Oh God, she thought, he's thinking I'm some sort of weird stalker or something. She almost tumbled off her stool as she leaned down quickly to lift up her camera bag.

"I'm a photographer, a photojournalist really, on assignment for Geographic Insight Magazine. I'm documenting life on the Great Plains."

He smirked.

"I see. But what has that got to do with taking my picture?"

She felt her face heat.

"I'm shooting people as well as scenery to give a sense of the true feel of this place."

Beau shook his head again.

"Sorry. I'm not one for posing in front of the camera, especially if the pictures are going to be published some place."

"But you're the perfect specimen," she blurted.

Specimen. Did I just say specimen? Her mind raced. Perfect Camilla, now you sound like some cold-hearted scientist who wants to put this guy inside a glass jar.

"Well, I didn't...what I meant," she stammered, "was that you're so representative of the Great Plains. You look like what women think cowboys look like."

Well, that just sounded lame.

"Women," she tried to explain, "I mean city women, always picture these super handsome cowboys and you're perfect for showing they really exist."

Oh God, she cringed. Can I just dig myself a deeper hole? Beau looked at her like she'd just done something stupid like stuck her hand in a beehive or swallowed a live fish. What's wrong with me, she wondered. Via rudimentary signs and gestures, she'd negotiated with basically uncivilized tribes in New Guinea and talked them into letting her take their picture. But she couldn't seem to speak, with any real nonhumiliating common sense, to this perfectly civilized and polite guy smack dab in the almost middle of the United States.

Handsome. I just called him super handsome.

Camilla wanted to run and hide. Instead, she leaned back against the counter to appear casual and non-flustered and promptly knocked over her chocolate milk, sending the glass flying in the air and shattering at Beau's feet. If she hadn't already felt like a deer in headlights, she sure felt like one now. People were staring. She was making a huge spectacle of herself.

"I'm sorry, Camilla," Beau said politely, kindly not acknowledging her flying glass incident. "Honestly, I just don't like having my picture taken."

Sliding off the stool to carefully pick up the largest pieces of broken glass on the floor as she collected her thoughts, she had no idea that it was too late. When she straightened and looked around again, Beau was gone. Wonderful, she grunted, mortified. It didn't make her feel any better when Sally promptly showed up beside her with a mop, dustpan, and broom to clean up her mess.

"Sorry, didn't mean to give you extra work," she muttered.

Sally scowled, saying nothing as she cleaned, but returned a few minutes later with a fresh glass of chocolate milk and her meal. Her appetite was now pretty much gone; Camilla struggled to at least appear casual and calm. Not like the fool I've just made of myself, she pined. For a second, she considered pulling out her phone and calling Ann right away but then decided against it. Everyone around her would hear her conversation, and she'd already made enough of an idiot of herself. So, she suffered in silence, overanalyzing her situation again and again with every bite of her steak. Stop it, she finally told herself. It's not like you'll see any of these people, or Beau, again. But anyway she thought about it, she was still mortified.

Three

AFTER RUNNING a few errands in town, filling up on gas and visiting Clay, an old high school friend who'd moved to Keenesburg, Beau got back on the highway to head home. He and Clay had a good laugh about the woman at the diner who wanted to take his picture so badly. Not that Beau wasn't used to easily garnering attention from the opposite sex. He'd managed that without even trying from the time he hit grade school. Even there, although he'd been just a kid, the little girls in his class had flocked to him, fawned over him, and brought him licorice and other types of candy, trying hard to be his friend. Female attention had burgeoned in high school and by the time he'd joined the football team, it was basically out of control. The cheerleaders had been the worst. Since they had something in common with him by way of the game, they'd all felt entitled to date him, especially because he was the most valuable player on the team.

Switching lanes as he pondered, Beau laughed out loud at his skilled ability to remain single. Not that he hadn't had more than his fair share of girlfriends but, at thirty-eight years old, he still hadn't found the one and tied the knot. He was in no rush. Living as an eligible bachelor suited him just fine. He had his ranch, his dogs, and lots of loyal friends. Of course, he dated on occasion, but romance wasn't his top priority. In short, he'd grown accustomed to the single life, throwing himself into his work before relaxing with friends, and he couldn't imagine giving his current lifestyle up. He thought about Camilla again and how she'd been different from any other woman he'd ever met. Certainly, she was just as pretty, if not more so. But she was also modest and unassuming, with a touch of innocence, which was rare. For sure she'd found him attractive, but she hadn't thrown herself at him. Smiling widely as he remembered her embarrassment, he realized he now regretted not spending a little more time with her.

"Super handsome," he said out loud, laughing. "She called you super handsome, buddy. Guess you're even charming enough for the city slicker gals."

But he'd already known that, he realized, thinking back on his business trip. He'd flown to Oklahoma City, Oklahoma for a series of cattle auctions to purchase some specially imported cows and another bull. In between the sales, he'd had a bunch of business meetings and dinners. His colleagues had done their best to introduce him to the most eligible women in their circle, and all the women had been overjoyed to meet him. Though he'd been polite and debonair, there'd been no spark on his end. Not that he specifically had anything against city women – he was sure some would adapt just fine to rancher life – it was just that the city's fast-paced lifestyle and pretentiousness usually presented an extra barrier to long-term compatibility and companionship.

He was still musing about his effect on women, and the inherent joys of single life, when a light gray Hyundai Accent sped by him, much closer to his vehicle than he liked, despite his comfort with highway travel. Thinking the driver was going to clip the side of his truck, he swerved to the right to avoid the car and laid his hand on the horn.

"Jesus! When will the idiots from the city learn to drive?!"

Although it just as easily could have been a country dweller on the way somewhere, his vast experience with highway driving told him that this probably wasn't the case. It took him a few moments to catch his breath and recover from the close call. Normally, nothing much unnerved him. After all, his daily chores included avoiding the horns of angry bulls and the trampling of angry cows protecting their calves. This, however, for some reason, pissed him off more than the other dangers he routinely dealt with. The majority of car accidents were avoidable and, most often, were caused by drunks behind the wheel or distracted drivers texting or talking and not paying attention to the road. I'll be so glad to get away from all this crap and back home to my ranch, he thought.

His mind wandered back to the auctions, and he smiled. He'd spent a fortune on his new acquisitions, but it was money well spent. His current beef cattle were already among the very best and highest priced on the market. And this addition of new blood would bolster his already amazing success. Smirking, he realized that city people would refer to him as some sort of cattle tycoon, and he supposed he was. People back home didn't have such rigid divisions as far as occupations and social class go. They just thought of him as Beau. That's what he loved about working and living in a small, tight-knit community. In many ways, they were all like one huge, extended family. Even the odd man or woman out was considered family, even if they were the black sheep of the bunch.

Laughing at the memory, he recalled that his own mother had referred to him as the black sheep at least a few times, not despite his business success but precisely because of it. Now, don't you go spending all your time with your cattle and counting all your money instead of finding some deserving woman to make into a wife. Your brothers have all given me grandchildren and honestly, Beau, I never thought you'd be the black sheep who didn't give me grandchildren to love. He still shook his head at that one. Of course, he'd come up with every rational reason for remaining unwed and childless, but his mom had simply labeled these excuses. Family, when it boiled down to it, she said, is what mattered the most. And dwelling on it now, as he had many times before, Beau acquiesced that she was right. If he ever met the right woman, he mused.

He'd driven a few miles up the highway, heavily lost in thought, when he noticed the same Hyundai Accent pulled over on the shoulder at the side of the road. Even from far away, he could see there was a woman standing beside it, kicking one of the back tires. She probably had a flat. He was shocked as he drove closer. It was Camilla from the diner. Well, wasn't this a bizarre stroke of luck. Luck, or something else.

She'd almost run him off the road. Glancing at the clock on his dashboard, he grunted. His flight back had been turbulent, Denver International Airport had been a madhouse, and he'd really been looking forward to getting home. Despite her marked lack of highway driving skills, he couldn't just leave her there to fend for herself.

He hit his blinkers to move out of the passing lane into the right lane so he could pull off the road. As inattentive and unaccommodating as always, numerous drivers ignored his intentions and sped by, not letting him into their lane. By the time he managed to pull off the highway, he was a little less than half a mile up the road.

"Here goes," he mumbled under his breath as he scrambled out of his truck.

With any luck, she had a spare, and he wouldn't have to drive her anywhere or stay with her until a tow truck arrived. It was a little windy, and the highway noise prevented her from noticing him as he ran toward her. She didn't see him until he startled her when he reached her car. She spun around and screamed. He chuckled.

"Need some help?" his smile widened.

Four

REALIZING she looked like a deer in headlights, yet again, Camilla did her best to restore a placid and unemotional look on her face. Just great. Out of all the people in this neck of the woods that could have stopped to help her, it had to be the guy she just made a huge fool of herself in front of. What were the odds? And what the hell was he doing here anyway? He'd left the diner long before her. He must have stopped somewhere, she rationalized, before getting on the road. These thoughts raced through her mind as she struggled to compose herself, taking much longer to answer his simple question than she would have liked.

"Sure," was all she could muster.

She turned her head away to gaze into the distance, realizing she felt so stupid by the fact that she had trouble looking him in the eyes. Thankfully, he either didn't notice or didn't care. He quickly strode by her and knelt down at the rear of her car.

"Looks like you ran over something. Got a spare?"

"I don't know," she said, then quickly elaborated, realizing she sounded dumb. "I assume so. This is a rental. I didn't look."

"Uh, huh..." he mumbled as he stood back up.

Jesus, he still thinks I'm some sort of an idiot! Feeling her face flush, Camilla struggled for words.

"Let me grab the rental agreement. I'm sure the company provides roadside assistance. At least I think so. Hang on while I grab my purse."

"Grab the keys."

She looked at him in wonder.

"At least, if you want me to change your tire if there's a spare. I need to open the trunk."

"Oh, right!" she blurted, feeling increasingly foolish all over again.

Why was he having this effect on her? She quickly leaned into the car, pulled the keys from the ignition, and handed them to him. He took them wordlessly, expressionless. Fantastic, she cringed. By all appearances, it sure didn't seem like he wanted to be there. About the only thing at that moment she could think of that was worse than being a fool, was being a helpless fool who was also a burden. She realized she'd never, ever, felt like this before. She was about to tell him that if he hadn't stopped, she would have easily had the situation under control—roadside assistance. A tow truck or just someone working for the towing company sent to change her tire. But she stopped herself before she said a word. What the hell am I thinking, she asked herself. I don't have to redeem myself in his eyes or explain anything to him.

Now that she considered it, she realized she knew nothing about this disarming guy at all. For all she knew, he wasn't the perfect gentlemanly cowboy that he seemed. She'd traveled the world in her photographic adventures and had seen enough of humanity to know that good looks, even fantastic looks, could deceive. She winced at how quickly she'd just handed her keys over to this handsome, virtual stranger. Good going, Camilla. Toss safety precautions to the wind for a smooth-talking, attractive face. If he was thinking much about their situation at all, he didn't show it. He'd opened her trunk while she stood pondering and was just pulling the spare tire out. Despite her continued discomfort, she wandered over.

"We didn't really finish introducing ourselves at the diner. I'm Camilla Santos, in case you were wondering. I can't remember if I even told you my name."

She held out her hand awkwardly for a handshake. He smirked and took it.

"Beau Rivers," he grunted as he threw the tire down on the ground and began to walk away.

What? Where was he going? What did I do or say wrong now? her mind screamed.

"Be right back," he called over his shoulder. "I've got tools in my truck."

Right. Way to go, Camilla. Lucky you didn't panic and call after him. By the time he returned, car jack and toolbox in hand, she'd more or less pulled herself together. At least enough, she hoped, that he didn't notice anything had been amiss with her. Actually, as he jacked up the car and then pulled off the flat tire, he didn't pay any attention to her at all.

"I really appreciate this," she said, moving a little closer to him as he worked.

"No problem," he insisted, not even looking up at her.

After a few moments of awkward silence, she decided to make better use of her time and take some pictures of the landscape around them. Looking around, she surmised she'd get some great shots of the mountains in the distance and the fields of crops by the side of the road if she stood next to the ditch to the right of her car. The sky was still an azure blue in the late afternoon sunlight and small, fluffy patches of clouds hung above the mountain peaks. After a few minutes, she became so absorbed in her work that she forgot all about Beau and her car and concentrated only on getting the best angles and shots. Unsure of what these crops were, she took multiple pictures of the fields anyway. She could check later what she'd documented growing if she decided to use these photos and there was a need for that.

Just as she lowered her camera, she was startled by the loud, piercing cry of a Bald Eagle circling and soaring high above the fields. Quickly lifting her camera and focusing, she managed to capture some fantastic close-ups of the bird. It was hunting, she realized. Scanning the fields far below it for small rodents to eat. If it managed to get one while she watched, that would be an awesome shot. Luckily, when it came to photography, patience was her virtue. She stood quietly, never taking her eyes off the predator as it looked for prey. Marveling at how raptors could possibly see things as tiny as mice from such a great height, she gasped as the bird suddenly dove downwards at incredible speed. With hardly a stir when it landed, it quickly ascended again, a tiny hare clutched tightly within its large talons. She refocused her camera to capture its successful departure with its meal.

Wow. She smiled, knowing her editor would really love these pictures. Maybe getting a flat tire wasn't such a bad thing after all. Suddenly remembering Beau, she turned toward her vehicle just as he stood up.

"What the hell do you think you're doing?" he quipped.

"What? What do you mean?" she was shocked.

"I told you at the diner, no photos of me," he raised his voice as he strode angrily toward her.

She froze for a second, unsure of what he was going to do. She'd run across the odd angry potential subject during assignments, and it was never good.

"No pictures of you!" she blurted, holding her camera tightly to her chest. "I'll show you."

She quickly scrolled through all the photos she'd taken since arriving at Deno's, stopping after she showed Beau the outside shots she'd taken there.

"I took these right before I went in to eat," she huffed. "I'm a professional. Like I told you, I do this for a living. If someone tells me they don't want their picture taken, I don't take any pictures of them."

His expression softened. Was that contriteness on his face?

"My apologies," he offered quickly.

He'd misjudged her and felt terrible. Apparently, she really wasn't like other girls from the city, or actually, not like any other girl from anywhere he'd met so far. She was totally upfront, honest, and true to her word.

"Your spare's almost on," he announced, hoping to extinguish the hot fire of indignation still burning in her eyes.

"Great."

Her eyes remained heated.

"Come on, I'll show you," he suggested, gesturing for her to follow him back to her car.

She did, silently, and he couldn't help noticing her stance was rigid and guarded even when they got back to her vehicle. He knelt down and continued tightening the spare. Their lack of conversation was all the more awkward because they'd chatted so easily at the diner just a short time ago. Finally, realizing she wasn't about to say anything or renew their conversation of her own accord, he looked up at her briefly as he was working.

"Look, I'm sorry if I offended you. I guess I'm not accustomed to dealing with many honest people. I just got back from a business trip."

"I see."

He finally detected less of an edge to her tone.

"Yup. Flew into Oklahoma City to buy some cattle, a couple dozen new cows and another bull."

"Really?"

He noted with satisfaction that her eyes had widened.

"Where are they? You're not bringing them back with you?"

"Having them trucked."

"Oh," she nodded.

"Why did you have to travel all that way? I mean, aren't there cattle closer to you somewhere?"

"Sure," he smiled, "Just not the ones I want."

He explained the importance of excellent bloodlines, and of obtaining cattle that were regularly health tested and screened for genetic and other defects. And that his trip also entailed securing future buyers when it was time for some of his herd to head to market.

"Impressive," she nodded. "I hadn't realized that raising beef was so complicated."

"It is, if you want to be successful at it," he smiled. Noting she was finally smiling too, he continued, "So there you go. I'm a rancher. I not only look like what women think cowboys look like, I'm a real cowboy just like you thought."

"The real deal," she smirked.

"Yup, for what it's worth."

They continued chatting casually as she watched him finish up with the spare tire. He scooped up her keys from the ground beside him and handed them back to her.

"Thanks so much."

"My pleasure."

Then, instead of gathering up his tools and walking away, he surprised her.

"Now, because you've been so respectful of my being camera shy, I suppose I will let you take my picture. But," he jokingly waved his finger at her, "only if you promise from the bottom of your heart that it won't end up an internet meme."

She burst out laughing.

"That, I can guarantee! Well, so long as no one scoops it off the pages of Geographic Insight Magazine."

They both laughed at that. He said he supposed it was a risk he was willing to take. At first, his poses were somewhat wooden and awkward. She could tell he hadn't been exaggerating in the least when he'd told her he didn't like being in front of the camera. Little by little, she got him to relax. At first, she took a few shots of him working on her tire. He pretended he was still tightening bolts. Afterward, she had him stand near the ditch, about where she'd been standing, taking pictures of the mountains and the eagle.

"Relax," she encouraged. "Just kind of look off into the distance like you're pondering something important. You know, deep in thought kind of thing."

He obediently gazed at the distant mountains, but his expression was still rigid and fake.

"Think of something that's important to you," she instructed. "Something or things you care a lot about. Your ranch. Your cattle. Everything you love about your home."

These instructions seemed to do the trick, and slowly, she watched Beau's expression and stance transform. His light green eyes actually seemed more vivid. His expression softened even as his gaze took on a more fervid edge. He stood taller, prouder, and suddenly appeared more assured and confident. Bold, daring, and measuredly reckless. Now he truly looked like every woman's cowboy dream.

"Perfect," she said, "Now just turn your head sideways a little to the left and lift your gaze a touch higher. Exactly. You got it!" she cheered him on.

She truly loved it when her subject got into the photos and enjoyed the process as much as her. For the next few minutes, she had him turn, facing in the other direction and repeating the same poses and gaze. Then, suddenly, she had another great idea.

"Hey, why don't we go over to your truck?" she asked. "Every great cowboy has a truck," she laughed.

"Why not?" he smirked, all the while amused at what she'd been able to talk him into.

After leaning casually on the back of the truck for a few shots, he came up with some better ideas for the rest of the photos himself. He dropped the tailgate, leaning back into it supported by his hands. Then, he sat on top of it, as if maybe someone else was driving and he was about to go for a ride that way. Finally, she took what seemed like an endless number of photos of him in the cab. Some of him reposing casually, leaning back against the seat, cheerfully looking at the camera, others with him looking straight ahead as if he was driving, his hands on the wheel.

"Fantastic! I can't thank you enough," she said when they were done. "The issue will be out in three months. I usually can't guarantee to anyone that their photos will make the editor's final cut, but I'm really certain yours will make it in."

He smiled.

"Thank you too, for calling me super handsome earlier," he winked.

Oh. My. God. She couldn't believe he actually took such notice of that, and that he was mentioning it now. Her face flushed from embarrassment, and she wanted to crawl away and disappear. Instead, she murmured an awkward "You're welcome," and listened to him chuckling as she scurried away, back to her car. She couldn't get in and disappear from his view fast enough. But, she realized, as she got behind the wheel, he'd already driven off long before she'd made it back to her vehicle. Thank God for that. He couldn't see her sitting there like a deer in headlights once again.

What the hell are you doing, Camilla, she asked herself. Who really cares what he thinks? She reached for her purse, fumbled inside it for a few seconds, and grabbed her cell. Scrolling quickly, she jabbed her finger on Ann's phone number and sat anxiously while listening to it ring.

"Hey," just the sound of her best friend's voice was comforting.

"Kill me now," she pleaded.

Laughing, Ann asked her what was wrong.

"What isn't?" Camilla's voice bordered on a shriek. "So, I actually did meet a hot and rich rancher. And no, sorry, I have no idea if he has a brother. But..."

"Are you already in Wyoming? Did you check into your hotel in Cheyenne?"

"What? No, I haven't even made it that far yet. I'm still in Colorado. I stopped for a bite to eat at a diner in Keenesburg and met the cowboy of every girl's dream."

"And you're upset, why?" Ann couldn't stop laughing.

"Because I made an absolute fool of myself!"

She went on to tell her how Beau had rescued her from the incredibly rude waitress and incomprehensible menu and how he'd outright refused to have his picture taken afterward. By the time she got to the flying glass incident and chocolate milk splurting through the air, her friend was in stitches and barely able to breathe.

"Well, don't worry too much about it, girlfriend. You're not likely to see this guy anywhere again."

"I just spent the last half hour or so taking a zillion photos of him."

"What?!" Ann screamed.

"Yeah, he came to my rescue when I had a flat tire..."

"Oh no!" Ann squealed. "This is starting to sound like the plot of some cheesy romance movie."

"Stop it! I know," Camilla agreed. "Anyway, I was so shocked to see him that I made a complete and utter fool of myself again when he offered to change the tire."

She filled Ann in on the whole scenario, ending her pitiful story with Beau thanking her for calling him super handsome before driving off into the sunset in broad daylight.

"This is just my luck," Camilla whined.

"Need I even say it? Two whole entire chances to impress him and you blew them both."

"Thanks for rubbing it in."

"Sorry," Ann laughed. "But hey, listen, the good news is that this time you're really not likely to see this guy anywhere again. I mean, what are the odds, right?"

"Are we talking for a normal, average person or for me?" Camilla finally laughed.

"Even for you," Ann snickered.

"Fine. Guess you're right. But just to be on the safe side, I'm sitting here by the side of the road until I'm sure he's driven a long, long way away. No way am I running the risk of seeing that dude again."

"Odds are remarkably slim to none," Ann reassured her.

"Yeah, well I'd prefer less of the slim and all of the none."

They spent the next ten minutes talking about what Camilla planned to do on the hopefully less embarrassing remainder of her trip. By the time they ended their conversation and Camilla pulled back out onto the highway, she was thoroughly convinced that in no way would she ever run into Beau Rivers again.

Five

BEAU GROANED IN RELIEF, sighing as he pulled into his incredibly long and winding driveway. Home sweet home, at last. Driving up the herringbone paving stones toward his sprawling ranch house, he realized that as much as he enjoyed business trips, with the excitement of buying the best cattle at auctions and arranging future sales, he loved his much less complicated life at home even more. Sure, the work never ended, and he often toiled from dawn to dusk. But at least here, everything was straightforward, more or less. Except for the odd surprise of a cow birthing early or an unprovoked charging bull, his days were pretty much predictable. And he could always totally be himself. Not that he ever put on a social mask or misrepresented himself. Just that he could be more relaxed at home and enjoy being who he truly was.

It seemed that city folk were always judging him, albeit sometimes without even meaning to. They were either overly mesmerized by his down-home-on-the-ranch lifestyle or envious of his wealth that it accrued. Or both. Even other cattlemen he met with on business out of town had an ambitious edge to their friendliness. Competition and success were everything to them. To me too, in a way, Beau surprised himself by thinking as he climbed down from his truck. Scanning his extensive fields of placidly grazing cattle warmed by the last of the late afternoon sun, he acknowledged that success was important to him too. If not for the same reasons, then for different ones. He wasn't obsessed with rivalry or money, but he took great pride and comfort in his well-established, stable and secure home. Ranching wasn't just his source of income; it was his life and in his blood.

Grinning as he inserted his key into the lock on his front door, he expected the heartwarming sounds of paws padding excitedly behind the door. Despite what his mother said about the downfalls of no one ever being home to greet him, he never felt unwanted or alone when he arrived. His three Border Collies were always incredibly thrilled to see him, and his numerous ranch hands always welcomed him with lots of updates and genuine smiles. When he heard no movement behind the door and saw only the empty foyer when he opened it, he surmised that his dogs were outside somewhere in the backyard, or the fields, or near the barns with Joe. Wheeling his suitcase only as far as the staircase, he left it to take upstairs later as he headed for the kitchen to place his cell phone on the charger.

The gray ceramic-tiled floors were spotless, marble countertops gleaming, with not a dirty cup or dish in sight. His housecleaners, as always, had done a fantastic job of keeping things in order while he was away. Glancing at his phone as he plugged its charger into the outlet, he noted that the alert for the dozen missed calls remained. While he normally answered his cell on business trips when he was available to speak, he'd strategically ignored these, preferring instead to deal with them once he returned home. All had been from the organizers of Cheyenne's Frontier Days festivities, and he already knew what they wanted. To know how much time he had on his hands and how he'd like to help. While he didn't shy away from his town's celebrations, he always preferred to keep his activities minimal because he didn't like all the fuss. He noticed that the light on his wall-mount landline was flashing. Its voicemail probably contained more calls from them.

Instead of checking messages, he strode to the fridge and grabbed a cold beer. Frontier Days could wait, but his dogs couldn't. He'd spent the last few days looking forward to seeing them. Expecting to have to wander around to find them, he was happy to step out onto the deck and see them sitting obediently for the treats that Joe was doling out to them.

"Hey boss, you're back!" his ranch manager saw him a second later. The dogs, unable to contain their excitement, abandoned their sit command and raced over.

"Shit, sorry, been working on honing their training," Joe laughed apologetically.

"No problem," Beau murmured as he squatted, gently pushing the slobbering dogs a little further away as they enthusiastically licked his face.

Homecomings like these left him wanting for nothing.

"And who says I'm not appreciated?!" Beau laughed as he stood back up, still petting his dogs as they jumped and circled excitedly around him.

"Someone said you're not appreciated?" Joe looked puzzled.

"Just mom," Beau grinned. "She keeps telling me that I need a wife to come home to, not my ranch hands and dogs."

"Well, yeah," Joe laughed. "I can sure see Ellie tryin' to drive that point home."

He'd worked for Beau's father, Hank, for decades before taking the position with Beau more than ten years ago. He knew the entire Rivers family as well as he did his own and had become close friends with all of them. Recalling how Ellie had even badgered him to find a good woman when he first took employment in his late teens, he chuckled. Ellie had been thrilled for him when he'd finally begun courting Harlene, never having a bad word to say about her, up until the time of his divorce. Even then, she'd insisted Harlene's main flaw had been her lack of appreciation for large families and not wanting kids. Joe hadn't had the heart to tell her that it was him who'd balked at having children, if only because he knew that Harlene wouldn't make a good mother. Her self-absorbed vanity and selfishness had precluded that. In any case, Joe recalled as he joined Beau at the patio table for a drink, he sure hadn't desired to be the one to burst Ellie's fantasy bubble about wives and large families fixing everything.

"How was your trip?" he asked as he took a drink from his beer that he'd had with him on the deck.

He was more family than ranch manager and Beau had always encouraged him to make himself at home.

"Fantastic trip for me, but more work now for you," Beau smirked. "Bought twenty-six of the best Wagyu cows in all the U.S. and a pretty feisty, by the looks of him, Angus bull."

"Ah, you're just tryin' to keep me on my toes," Joe grinned. "Well, rest assured, good buddy, that if it ever gets too much for me, I'll just call on you for a little help."

They both broke into hearty laughter at that. The truth was, Joe was getting up there in age. Although it hadn't necessarily slowed him down much, there had been a few occasions when he'd asked for Beau's help. While many of the ranch's twenty-two hands were more than exceptionally experienced at their job, none were as skilled at solving everyday and larger problems and handling the cattle as well as their boss. Beau believed in a hands-on approach to running his ranch, which actually made it the smoothest operation in the whole state. He'd grown up with beef cattle and with his father constantly encouraging him to learn all about the business from literally the time he could walk and talk. As a result, Beau was not only adept at the ins and outs of everyday chores, but he also kept a close, eagle eye on his ever-evolving and growing business to the advantage of everyone involved.

"When they arrivin?" Joe asked him, mentally preparing a to-do list as he talked.

"The bull will get here in four days, providing he passes all additional health checks. The cows, I think all of them should be here within about a week."

"Right on. We'll be ready," Joe smiled. "Anything else exciting happen this trip? The boys down there still tryin' to match you up?"

"Yup," Beau's laughter was contagious. "Seems just about every one of them had just the perfect gal for me."

"And?" Joe leaned forward inquisitively. "No luck?"

Beau shook his head.

"Not like I was worried about it. You know me, Joe. Getting hitched is just about the last thing on my mind. I mean, there was nothing wrong with any of the women I met through the guys in Oklahoma. It's just that there wasn't anything right either."

"Yeah, yeah..." Joe's voice trailed off in deeper thought about his own bachelorhood.

"But," Beau smiled. "I did at least meet one woman who was different than any girl I've ever met before."

"Different?" Joe cocked his head. "You mean in a good way?"

"Yeah," Beau laughed again. "At least I think so. If nothing else, she was really amusing, and it broke up the usual tedium and monotony of my trip."

"Was she at the auctions?" Joe asked.

"Nope. No way. She's a city slicker through and through."

"Thought you weren't real partial to those," Joe's eyes narrowed.

"I wasn't...I'm not," Beau corrected himself but couldn't help the sudden buoyancy in his mood as he told Joe all about Camilla.

How he'd run into her at Deno's in Keenesburg. Or more accurately, how she'd literally run into him, bashing into his side with her camera bag. How he had rescued her, well, actually rescued the incredibly rude waitress from her wrath. When he got to the part of his story where Camilla tried desperately to talk him into letting her take his picture, Joe leaned back in his chair and eyed him incredulously.

"Sounds weird to me. Shit, more than weird. Don't tell me she's some sort of stalker-type female. You know, one of those fatal attractions..."

"No, hell no," Beau laughed. "Just a photojournalist on assignment for Geographic Insight Magazine, documenting the Great Plains. She said I look like what cowboys are supposed to look like, or something strange like that. She called me a perfect specimen," he laughed harder. "Said that city women picture super handsome cowboys, and she needed my photo because it would be perfect to prove they really exist!"

"Get out..." Joe snorted. "She actually said that?"

"Yup. Pretty much right before she accidentally sent her chocolate milk flying off the counter with the glass shattering right at my feet."

Joe was in hysterics, laughing so hard he couldn't breathe.

"And you kept a straight face?" he stammered between bouts of laughter.

Beau nodded and grinned.

"I couldn't have done it..." Joe snickered. "I'd have busted a gut laughing right there."

Recalling Camilla's shock and embarrassment, and how endearingly she'd blushed, Beau explained how he'd politely turned down her photo request and gotten out of the diner as quickly as he could. Only to run into Camilla again a little later.

"No way?! Please tell me she didn't follow you," Joe's eyes widened.

"She did," Beau nodded again. "But totally by accident."

Joe wasn't convinced until he explained that he'd dropped by his friend Clay's for a bit before getting on the highway and Camilla had come up speeding behind him.

"Didn't know it was her though, at that point. Her Hyundai just about sideswiped me and almost sent me careening off the road."

"Damn..."

"I knew it must have been a city slicker but didn't know it was her until I got a little ways ahead and saw her with a flat tire pulled over at the side of the road."

"Don't tell me," Joe snickered. "You pulled over, didn't you buddy?"

Surprised at his embarrassment in admitting it, Beau said yes.

"Well, hell, I couldn't just leave her there. What if she didn't know where to call for a tow truck? Besides, there's more than a few roadside predators out there just searching for women having car problems. Anything could have..."

"So, your excuse is you had to rescue the damsel in distress?"

Joe's smirk was infectious.

"In a way, yeah. But it gets more amusing..."

"Couldn't possibly," Joe burst into another round of laughter.

"I was changing her tire and thought she was sneaking pictures of me, so I freaked out. Went stomping over and literally accused her until she showed me the shots in her digital camera. I felt so shitty about upsetting her that I let her take a few photos of me before I left."

"A few?" Joe raised his eyebrow. "As in how many?"

Shaking his head in disbelief as Beau recounted all his poses, Joe controlled himself until the end of the description of the photoshoot.

"And they're going to be in this geographic magazine, she said?"

"Geographic Insight, yeah. Camilla said she was sure they'll make the editor's final cut."

"I see," Joe was chuckling again. "Not only are you a knight in shining armor, but you're also a male model too."

"Very funny," Beau snickered. "From what she told me, it's a big feature piece, so if anything, there'll be one or two small shots of me."

"Not if Camilla gets her way," Joe hadn't stopped laughing. "By the sounds of it, bud, she'll be talking her editor into putting you on the cover!"

"Not a chance, but hell, at least Camilla provided me with my amusement for the day."

He was laughing as hard as Joe when his friend's expression turned mischievous.

"Don't laugh," Joe blurted. "With your crazy luck, this woman's probably the one and if she ever finds out you were laughing at her, one way or the other, she'll make you pay."

"Well, for all that to happen, Camilla would have to see me again. I highly doubt that's ever going to happen. In any case," Beau sank back in his chair, "I think I'm actually relieved. She was pretty. And really nice and all in an innocent kind of way. But let's face it, she was more than a little bit klutzy and kind of odd."

"Uh huh..." Joe's amused smile remained.

They chatted a little more about women in general, which naturally led Joe to the topic of Carolyn from Frontier Days. She was on the festival's committee and had been calling Joe repeatedly, urging him to have Beau call her back as soon as possible.

"Says it's important," Joe told him. "And to tell you the truth, she's been driving me and other people crazy looking for you."

Beau grunted and rolled his eyes. Every year it was the same thing. He'd known Carolyn since high school, and she wasn't the type to give up when she really wanted something. And lucky for me, Beau winced, I always seem to be at the top of her list. Even though he figured he'd rather be unarmed, facing a charging Angus bull at any given moment than acquiescing to Carolyn's demands, he decided it was easier to at least call her back to see what she wanted this time. It wasn't like she'd disappear anytime soon. Sighing and reluctantly pushing his chair back from the table, he went into the house to grab his phone. I just know I'm going to regret this, he thought, as he clicked on her number. I suppose it could be worse, he mused, as he listened to it ring. But for the life of him, he couldn't figure out how.

Six

NOT LONG AFTER SUNDOWN, Camilla rolled into Cheyenne. She was more than a little tired from her long drive; not to mention the stress of her flat tire, and her recurring embarrassment from making a fool of herself – not once, but twice – in front of Beau. As she turned left onto Gardenia Avenue, following the directions of her GPS, she told herself for the hundredth time not to worry about it. It was over with. She wasn't likely to see him again. What I need right now, she mused, is a long, hot shower and to plan some of tomorrow's activities. She wanted to get photos of literally everything she could as the Frontier Days festivities got underway. Guessing others didn't want to miss anything either, she noticed that traffic was insane for a small town as she made her way to her hotel. The pamphlet her editor had provided mentioned that people flocked to Cheyenne for this yearly celebration from miles around.

Praying the Wayfair Inn hadn't screwed up her reservation – that had happened to her more than once on her photography trips – she spotted it up ahead. It was only a block from downtown. If nothing else, its location was convenient. She had no idea what the rooms were like. Smirking and remembering one of her visits to Africa, she comforted herself that at least, this time, she wouldn't be roughing it for a few days, literally taking shelter and sleeping in a safari hut. There were only a few parking spaces left in the lot, and she quickly slipped into one. So far so good. She mentally kept her fingers crossed as she strode through the front doors with her bags. The lobby was nothing fancy, about as lackluster as the look from the outside. But it was tidy and clean.

Smiling at a group of children running around in circles as the adults they were with chatted nearby, Camilla walked to the front desk. She hadn't truly realized how tired she was until she held her breath as the clerk searched the computer for her reservation. Please, please have my room, she prayed. The flat tire, and oh yeah, she winced as she remembered the shattered glass of chocolate milk at Deno's, was the only bad luck she wanted to have today.

"Here it is, Miss Santos. You're very lucky you prepaid and requested late check-in. We're totally full with visitors for Frontier Days. We've had to turn numerous people away."

"I bet. Traffic was crazy as I drove through town. I take it the festival's very popular?"

"Oh, yes. We get booked up for months ahead of time!"

"Fantastic!" Camilla smiled. "I'm here to take photos of the activities for a national magazine."

"You won't be disappointed," the clerk assured her as she handed her the room's key card. "Oh, wait," she said as an afterthought, grabbing a few brochures and fliers at the side of the desk, "We've got lots of promo materials. These'll help you plan your time here and to decide what you want to do."

After thanking her, Camilla finally made it to her room.

"Ugh," she moaned. "Nothing fancy, but at least it has a queen-sized bed."

Realizing that, in her weariness, she was actually talking to herself, she laughed. At least she wasn't breaking things again. She noted the cups stacked on top of the small microwave were plastic. Well, that was good, just in case. She found her thoughts wandering to Beau again as she kicked off her shoes. Stop it, she chided, telling herself for the hundred and first time that she was never going to see that guy again. By the time she unpacked her suitcases, she was so tired that she almost decided to skip grabbing a bite to eat. Although tempted to just order up room service, she knew it was much more prudent to go out somewhere. Although the festivities weren't getting started until morning, she might get lucky and grab some more interesting photos. Grabbing her camera bag, she headed out the door.

It was after 9:00 p.m. by this point, and she was surprised to find the streets still packed with people. She stopped a young couple walking by her, hand-in-hand, and asked if they knew of a good place to eat.

"We just had dinner at Ranch Steakhouse, a few blocks up that way," the guy pointed.

"Okay, thanks," she did her best not to cringe as they walked away.

She could only handle so much steak, she thought as her mind raced back to Deno's, and of course, to who had recommended the steak to her there. Hoping there were other things on the menu, she headed in that direction. Luckily, she came upon a small café first with patio seating. It was packed with laughing and joking people, and she eyed the food hungrily as the waitress walked near her carrying delicious-looking plates of food. Looking above her at the lettering on the banner, she smiled. Red Barn Café it is. By the time her meal got to her table, she was chatting with Ann on her phone.

"Not a sign of him," she snickered, "so I think all of the glasses here are safe."

"Don't order chocolate milk, just in case," Ann joked.

"Way ahead of you, girlfriend. I'm sipping iced tea as we speak."

Ending their conversation by promising to check in with her tomorrow, Camilla dove into her cheddar chicken wrap. It was either the best food in Cheyenne or she was just super hungry. She didn't care either way. Although she kept scanning the café and the people walking by it on the street, she was disappointed that no one jumped out at her as being another perfect model for her assignment. Perfect model, she winced, recalling she'd told Beau he was a perfect specimen. Damn! Why couldn't she get this guy out of her mind? Laughing at herself as she finished her meal, she managed to refocus her thoughts. She browsed some of the brochures the hotel clerk had given her. Realizing that she had to wake up bright and early if she didn't want to miss anything, she asked for the check as soon as she'd finished eating. Her mundane hotel seemed more welcoming to her as she relished getting some sleep.

Tired as she was, that didn't happen right away. She tossed and turned in bed for at least half an hour, listening to people talking loudly and milling around on the street and even in the hallway outside her room. Her hot shower had relaxed her, but not enough to sleep through anything. Surprised at herself that she wasn't nodding off – she'd slept like a baby in war zones, after all – she refused to admit what else, or who else, could still be flitting in and out of her thoughts. By the time her cell's alarm awakened her in the morning, she was more than ready to leap out of bed and get on with her day. If the increased noise and activity outside and in her hallway were any indication, there was already a lot happening on the festival's first day. Encouraged by the country music blasting in the street as she got dressed and applied her makeup, she told herself, no more distractions. This was going to be a great day.

Dressed in casual slacks and a colorfully-flowered blouse, she realized her mistake as soon as she strode out the front doors of the hotel lobby. Her clothes stuck to her like glue. It was sweltering hot outside. She hadn't realized it with the air conditioning going in her room. No way could she concentrate on photos or anything else until she changed. As it turned out, changing was a good thing. She emerged wearing much more comfortable clothes after she'd relaxed in her room to cool off a bit. A light-yellow sundress and better walking shoes. About to grab one of her brochures to decide where to head first, she ran into the front desk clerk just walking back into the hotel.

"Hi there," she smiled, glad to see her. "Do you have a minute? I went through all the brochures and things you gave me but there's so much here that I'm a little confused about the best places to go and what to do first. What would you recommend?"

"Well, you're just in time to catch the main parade that's about to start. Head a couple of blocks down that way," she said as she pointed, "you'll see where the street's blocked off and you'll have a great vantage point. Make sure you go to Pinafore Park to check out all of the food tents. There's a map of everything here," she told Camille, tapping one of the brochures in her hands. "Make sure to take photos of the animals in the parade, and on display at Harrison Park. There's horses and cattle and other livestock. A dog show too. Drop by the car show a few blocks from there; it always has fancy cars and trucks and catch the kiddie parade later in the day."

"Wow, thanks!" Camilla smiled gratefully.

She'd get fantastic photos for sure. She thanked her again as she turned and began walking away, the clerk yelled after her.

"Almost forgot! Don't leave until you've seen all the musicians and bands. They'll begin performing a little later, in the main square where they've set up the stage. They're the highlight of the whole event."

"Great!" Camilla acknowledged.

Her editor was going to love her submissions. She rushed toward the barricaded area the clerk had mentioned, anxious not to miss even one float in the upcoming parade. She wasn't disappointed when it began. Seemingly stretching for miles, the parade started with a huge float displaying a twenty-foot-tall balloon of a cowboy merrily swaying to country music in the wind. Smiling and waving children of various ages, wearing their best western outfits, waved happily at the spectators as they rolled by. Each float seemed to be more creative than the last. Most were sponsored by local businesses, their banners waving high or hanging from the sides, but some also publicized local charities and clubs.

When the 4-H float arrived, it was met with enthusiastic cheers. The float itself was constructed to resemble a big red barn with a white picket fence around it. Farm animal statues and bales of hay and straw made up the decorations, but the best part was the most adorable animals that Camilla had ever seen. Tiny miniature horses, led by waving children, walked alongside the float, closely followed by alpacas also on leads, wearing tiny cowboy hats. Camilla snapped countless photos of not only the wonderful animals but also of the loudly cheering and waving crowd. At one point, when the parade stopped in front of her for a few minutes, Camilla snapped pictures of professional riders on horseback. They were dressage horses and danced to a medley of popular western songs.

One of the last floats to roll by, constructed by the Red Barn Café where she'd eaten last night, reminded her that the hotel clerk had told her to check out the food tents in Pinafore Park. She went there right after the parade ended, just in time for an early lunch. Overwhelmed by all the choices, she wasn't sure what to eat. Savory scents of sausages, burgers, pulled pork, beans, chili, and spareribs filled the air. After snapping photos of the vendors inside the tents and outside, underneath their colorful umbrellas, she finally settled on grilled sausage on a bun. It was surprisingly tasty for what amounted to fast food, and she considered getting a second helping before reminding herself that she still had a lot to see if she didn't want to miss anything. Consequently, she scanned the map within one of the brochures and headed to the livestock display at Harrison Park.

Photo opportunities abounded there. Not only of the horses, cattle, and other livestock but also of the adults and children displaying and viewing them. Staring up into the serene face of the largest horse she'd ever seen, Camilla was informed it was a Clydesdale, one of the most gentle and trainable breeds. A few display areas away, she took pictures of week-old piglets snuggled up with their mom. Most of the cattle were young, up to a few months old, she was told. One of her best shots depicted a Holstein calf drinking hungrily from a huge feeding bottle, held by a little boy no more than five or six years old. There were fancy chickens, breeds she'd never heard of, and all kinds of beautifully-colored ducks and even lambs at the far side of the huge shaded tent. When the speakers announced the forthcoming dog show, she rushed outside to grab some photos of it as well. A remarkably tiny teacup Chihuahua took first place in the small dog category, and a Great Pyrenees won the large dogs competition.

From there, Camilla hit the car show, which was only a few blocks away. She snapped over a hundred photos of impeccably clean and shiny fancy cars and trucks. By that point, it was time for the kiddie parade, which was about to begin close to downtown. She arrived just in time to photograph the first participants, adorable six to eight-year-old majorettes. Of course, this parade was much shorter than the main one earlier – many of the children were really young and could only walk so far. Although there were a few small floats, most of the kids strolled or danced by, although one group drove by on tricycles. Camilla almost couldn't believe the wonderful enthusiasm and passion that everyone, participants and spectators alike, had for the event. Honestly, she thought to herself, she'd never seen anything like it. Not at any competition or fair she'd taken photos of before. There really was something different and special about life in this part of America and the lifestyle within the Great Plains.

It was nearing four o'clock, and she decided to head to the main square for the bands and musicians, the highlight of the entire event. By the time she got there, the streets were even more congested than before. The vibe was amazing. People were really excited, and that excitement was contagious. She found herself looking forward to the performers. Despite her rough start to this assignment, it really wasn't going to be so bad after all. She glanced around at the countless people talking in small groups and meandering by. Cowgirls with cowboys, fancily-dressed locals, and even some obvious tourists strolling through the crowd. The stage was still empty; helpers were setting up, and the people were more than accommodating in posing for pictures as they waited for the entertainment to start. She'd just finished taking a few pictures of a smiling group of teens and refocused her camera for another shot of the crowd when she gasped at a familiar face through the lens. She lowered her camera for a better look, but there were far too many people. Beau had disappeared into the crowd.

Seven

"CHEER UP, BRO," Greg laughed. "You look like you're about to walk the plank!"

"I am," Beau laughed as he answered his brother. "You know how I feel about singing in public. How the hell did I ever let Carolyn talk me into this?"

He shook his head dejectedly as Greg laughed even harder.

"How does Carolyn talk anyone into anything? Perseverance and strong will and more stubbornness than any bull anyone in this whole entire county has ever run across."

Beau nodded. His brother was right. He sure wouldn't be chuckling like this, he noted, if he'd ever been the target of Carolyn's desires for anything. Three years older than him, Greg had been ahead of him and Carolyn all through school, therefore flying under her radar and easily avoiding her stalkerish tendencies. Nope, Beau grinned as he recalled, I've been the lucky one to consistently garner Carolyn's attention, long before I even made the football team to attract even more girls than before. In fairness, it wasn't that he hated or even disliked Carolyn; it was just that he didn't like her in the least. At least not in the way she wanted. His senior years in high school had been spent doing everything he could to avoid taking her out for even one date.

46

While many of his buddies had teased him about it, even back then, he'd insisted he wasn't the type to take advantage even when a girl threw herself at him. That didn't sit all too well with most of the football players on his team; most thought him crazy to not revel in his fantastic luck. Carolyn was as super attractive back then as she was now. It was just her personality and pushiness that got in the way of it all. When she'd finally started dating Jay, a football player from another high school, Beau had been more than relieved. Overjoyed when she announced her engagement, he literally would have jumped for joy if he hadn't controlled himself. She'd remained conspicuously flirty with him throughout her entire relationship with Jay. Now that she was divorced, it was game on again.

He looked up from untangling speaker wires when he heard the familiar sounds of Greg warming up on the piano. He smirked at how different his brother was from him. Greg loved performing and being in front of a crowd. If it was up to him, they'd be much more than a hobby garage band and would be booking gigs all over the state. This is why, Beau acknowledged, he'd given in to Carolyn when she'd begged him to play guitar and sing today. One of the booked bands had a scheduling conflict and there was absolutely no one with such short notice to fill the void.

"This the final song list, then?" Tyler approached him holding a sheet of paper.

"Yup, that's it. Go ahead and tape the lists up for us."

"Sure thing," Tyler smiled as he walked away.

One of the band's unofficial roadies, he was Greg's best friend. In fact, all of their volunteers and crew were buddies and relatives. It had never been worth hiring anyone officially since their gigs were few and far between. Although this, of course, rattled Greg, it was just the way Beau liked it. Playing at the odd wedding, family reunion, or town barbecue was fine with him. Anything more frequent would annoy him. Especially on a sweltering hot day like today. He'd just carried a bunch of equipment over to the far side of the stage and was grimacing as he wiped the sweat from his brow when Matt walked by him, chuckling.

"Heads up, bud. Predator approaching from your left."

Just great. He looked over to see Carolyn sashaying toward him yet again. How she managed to walk on those six-inch heels without falling flat on her face amazed him. Especially when the stage was littered with wires and stray microphones and other equipment all over the place. She'd caught his eye as he'd seen her coming so he couldn't get out of her line of fire this time and run away. He glanced around quickly, looking for something, anything to get behind, to keep her from getting too close to him. The speakers weren't near enough to dart to before she reached him. He cringed. Here it comes; he did everything he could not to physically flinch.

She was always touching him, placing her hand over his, patting his arm, nonchalantly stroking his shoulder, and worse, "accidentally" brushing her body against his.

"Hey, Beau," her beautiful smile gleamed with her lascivious, not-so-secret intentions. "Are you sure you want to open with this song?"

For the first time, he noticed the paper in her hand. His song list. She just couldn't stop constantly inserting herself into his business. She should be more than happy that I'm even here, he shrugged, realizing he didn't hide his dismay well enough. He tensed as she reached him, stopping literally inches from him and, of course, hooking her arm in his as she leaned into him to talk.

"What's the problem?" he asked, trying to diminish the harshness of his tone with a sudden forced smile.

"Well, I just thought that maybe you guys could begin with something, you know, more energetic than this."

He stepped back reactively. She stumbled forward because their arms were still hooked together, and she wasn't about to let go. Really?! This is how ladies feel, Beau winced, when overbearing men get into their space.

"What's wrong with the song, Carolyn?" he asked as politely as he could. "It's a crowd favorite. Everyone loves it."

"Well, yeah, I guess," she acquiesced. "I just like some of your songs so much better. Especially," she leaned into him, "the ones you wrote yourself."

"Greg wrote our opening song," he said defensively, "and he's a much better songwriter than I am."

"No one writes better songs than you," she smiled, laying it on real thick.

Yeah, sure he thought, running over an exceptionally long list of rich and famous country stars in his mind. He sighed. It was better not to argue with her or to really say much at all. Anything he said during any conversation just gave Carolyn an excuse to prolong it, and talking to her right now was just about the last thing he wanted to do. He hated all this hoopla to begin with, and if it was solely up to him, he'd much rather have spent the evening relaxing at home alone.

"Don't worry," he assured her, "the crowd will love our set."

He took a step backward again and, this time, managed to untangle himself from her arm.

"I'd better finish setting up," he eased into his effort to push her away.

She'd never been one to take a hint.

"Oh, well sure," she smiled again. "Don't let me hold you up."

Like you wouldn't dream of that, he thought, but murmured only "no problem," before nodding politely and walking away. He'd just successfully erased all annoying thoughts about her from his mind when Greg walked up beside him to help him with the speaker.

"I was about to toss you a life preserver to save you from drowning in a sea of love when she walked away," he laughed.

"Yeah, well next time," Beau smirked, "don't wait so damn long."

"Maybe I just love seeing my staunch bachelor brother squirm," he burst out laughing.

"Very funny. If all women were like her, I don't think any man on this planet would savor the married life for long."

"You probably got that right," Greg snickered as he walked away.

Easy for him to find this so amusing, Beau mused, as he finished setting up the speaker. His brother was happily married to a great woman and had three children, two boys and a girl. They were coming tonight, along with many of their other relatives. It seemed everyone loved joining in on the Frontier Days festivities except for him. His mind shifted to Camilla. She'd be here too, somewhere. Probably enjoying herself with the party atmosphere and getting great shots; at least, he smirked, if she didn't drop her camera and break it; she was such a klutz. He actually laughed out loud, remembering the flying glass of chocolate milk. Looking around quickly, he was glad that none of his crew noticed. They were already teasing him about Carolyn and loved to make fun of him whenever women were in the picture fawning over him.

Fawning. He smiled at the thought. Camilla had very obviously liked him. But she was sweet and not pushy. Jeez, his brother would have had a field day if he'd seen any of that. Even Joe had laughed harder at the situation than he'd ever seen him laugh. Well, as amusing as his encounter with Camilla had been, it was over and done with. He told himself to stop thinking about her. They'd had some fun moments while she took his pictures, but nothing had come of it. Which was probably for the best. He smirked again at how different she was than other women – even if it was in a nice way – and reminded himself that she wasn't from around here anyway. She would be going back home soon to her life in Baltimore.

"Beau?"

He bristled. It was Carolyn again, rushing toward him. He quickly got on the other side of the speaker to avoid her latching onto his hand or arm.

"Hi, sorry," she gushed unconvincingly. She wasn't sorry to be bothering him again at all. "I was just thinking that maybe after you're done your set, we could get together to discuss some of the other committees I'm on and things I organize."

"Why?" he said more abruptly than he'd intended.

She inched her way around the speaker, and he slowly slid in the other direction, trying to get away from her.

"You guys are always such a hit when you play, it would be wonderful if you could perform at some of my other events."

Oh, no, he cringed. Even if she hadn't been involved, more gigs were the last thing he wanted. It was lucky Greg hadn't arrived to rescue him yet because he'd jump at more opportunities to play.

"I don't think so, Carolyn. You know how busy I am with the ranch. Not that I wouldn't love to and all, but I just can't put too much on my plate."

Her pout would have been humorous if it wasn't so exaggerated. Instead, he did everything in his power not to cringe again.

"Well," she inched closer, "at least give me a chance to try and talk you into it. You might surprise yourself and change your mind when I tell you about everything I have planned."

Not a chance. He slid to the other side of the speaker to get farther away from her. Just about to voice another objection, he was saved from Carolyn's continued begging when Greg showed up.

"Hey, Carolyn. How's it going? Frontier Days keeping you hopping?"

"As always," she smiled, actually thrilled he'd come over to talk.

Not good, Beau dwelled. This could only lead to...

"I'm just trying to talk your brother into booking some more gigs at some of my other events."

Greg's face lit up. Beau groaned.

"Greg, we got to talk about this first," he insisted. "I don't have a lot of time and..."

Seeing a renewed opportunity to corner Beau into spending some time with her after the show tonight, she jumped in with vigor.

"I was just saying to Beau that we should get together after the show to discuss all of this. You have time tonight, right Greg? Bring Christie and the kids if you want. And Beau, of course."

Of course, Beau shrugged. If she couldn't get alone time with him, she'd settle for any time with him at all. Greg looked at him hopefully just as he slid up behind Carolyn, out of her view. He shook his head, no, as emphatically as he could. Thank God. He saw the lightbulb of realization go off in Greg's eyes.

"Not tonight, Carolyn, but we'll talk about it soon for sure."

She looked deflated, and even somewhat annoyed.

"I promise," Greg assured her, placing his arm around her shoulder as he casually led her away.

They were still talking a few minutes later when Beau looked up from tuning his guitar. What the heck were they speaking about for so long? He could just imagine the conversation. Carolyn desperately trying to set up some sort of lunch or dinner to talk about gigs, making sure that Beau would be in attendance. He tried hard to read the expression on his brother's face. Poor Greg, he concluded. He's trying to stay true to my wishes to avoid Carolyn and playing more gigs while also ignoring his own wishes to perform in public much more than they currently were. It was an uncomfortable tightrope of sorts for sure, and he didn't envy being in Greg's shoes. But, he admitted to himself, as awful as he felt about it, he almost didn't mind disappointing his brother about additional gigs if Carolyn was involved.

Feeling guilty about not feeling guilty enough by the time Greg returned to talk to him, Beau looked apologetically at his brother.

"Sorry, Greg. I know you wanna play more gigs and all, but you know how I feel about..."

"Feel about Carolyn and about public performances," Greg jumped in. "I know, I know. Don't worry. I told her we're both really busy with our ranches and that my kids keep me tied up with their sports and stuff. But," he smirked. "I'm not so sure she's about to give up."

Beau groaned.

"Sorry, it's just that I..."

"I get it, bro. Don't worry about it. Honestly, it's not that big of a deal."

"Okay," Beau nodded, looking past Greg into the crowd to make sure that Carolyn had wandered off.

He couldn't see her anywhere as he scanned the crowd milling around the stage and farther beyond. But his eyes widened when he thought he spotted another familiar face. A better one. A very pretty one. He couldn't believe his luck, if that was what it was. He was sure he'd just seen Camilla walking past a group of teenagers and disappearing again into the crowd.

Eight

CAMILLA LOOKED at the photo counter on her digital camera. She almost couldn't believe she'd already taken so many shots. But she shouldn't have been surprised. This often happened to her on assignments. Once she got rolling and really absorbed herself in it, her photos flowed so fast that she could scarcely keep up with her thoughts about who and what to take pictures of next. She was having a great time here. And her day hadn't even reached the main event yet, the musicians and bands. She glanced at her cell phone. It was still a little way off from when the first band was scheduled to begin so she decided to wander around and keep taking photos of people in the crowd. She'd found more than enough interesting children, young couples, and even large family groups that exuded the harmony and togetherness of life on the Great Plains. So rather than taking a break, she decided it was always best to get even more photos. Keeps my editors busy, she smiled. And, of course, keeps them impressed with my eye for quality shots and dedication to my job.

She looked around, trying to spot some interesting people and activities she hadn't noticed yet, when she realized she was squinting, and what – or more accurately who – she was really looking for. Beau had slipped into her thoughts pretty consistently as the day had worn on, especially because she was almost one hundred percent sure that it was really him she'd spotted earlier disappearing into the crowd. Is he here? she wondered, even as she chided herself for the thought. Here I go again, she snickered, thinking about someone who probably isn't thinking about me. She had an uncanny talent for that, she admitted. If she truly took the time to analyze all her past relationships, she hadn't always chosen the best men. And she hadn't always realized it until it was much too late in the game. Sure, her plentiful photography gigs had gotten in the way of romance, but her not always perfect judgment in men hadn't helped. For a second, she truly wished that Ann was with her. No matter where they went, they always had so much fun. Next best thing, she smirked, fishing in her camera bag to pull out her cell.

"Okay, let me guess," Ann laughed. "You ran into your favorite cowboy again, and this time you actually injured him when you accidentally broke another glass."

"No! Stop it," Camilla laughed. "He's safe. I assure you. For a second, I thought I saw him earlier, but it probably wasn't even him. Right now, I see absolutely no sign of him here."

"And...do I detect a tinge of disappointment in your voice?"

Rats. Ann knew her better than almost anyone. She was onto her.

"All right, whatever," Camilla giggled. "I admit he keeps crossing my mind. But it's not like I'm looking for him or anything. I've gone tons of places and already captured about a zillion great shots. Still have lots more to take before the day's over. It's still about another hour and a half before the main event."

"Main event?"

"Yeah, there's a bunch of bands playing tonight in the main square. I'm here now, snagging shots of people in the crowd."

"So, this festival's a huge thing, then?" Ann asked. "Sounds like it's much more fun there than you thought."

"Actually, it is," Camilla admitted, glad to get off the topic of Beau.

"So then, there is a chance that Frontier Days is so popular that Mr. Super Handsome is actually there and will cross your path again."

Camilla felt her cheeks heating up and hoped that no one standing near her noticed her blush.

"Oh, God, Ann. I've tried so hard to forget how badly I embarrassed myself by calling him that to his face."

"You're welcome," Ann laughed. "You need me to remind you to keep thinking about more than just your job."

"Ughh," she groaned. "Yeah, well, you just go ahead and do that once I return home to Baltimore, will you? I don't need any more distractions here."

"Hmmm," Ann huffed. "Okay, girlfriend. But call me if Mr. Distraction crosses your path again."

Camilla flinched and realized her heart was racing at the thought. Realizing she was creating her own distraction just by talking about Beau, she quickly decided to let Ann go and get back to work.

"Will do," she promised, snickering. They chatted happily for a few more minutes before hanging up.

Scanning the crowd again for more prospective, impromptu models, she mentally kicked herself for still looking for Beau, despite trying hard to appear nonchalant. This is getting ridiculous, Camilla, her inner voice nudged her in the ribs. You don't chase men. You never have, and this is no time to start. Sure, whatever, she continued her mental dialogue with herself. I can't chase someone who probably isn't even really here. Despite her continued reassurances to herself that she wasn't chasing, and this wasn't the case, she began to get mad at herself because it really was.

"Excuse me," a familiar voice startled her, and she just about jumped out of her skin.

It was the hotel desk clerk, out of uniform, so it took Camilla a moment to recognize her.

"Oh, hi. I didn't expect to see you here."

The girl laughed.

"I'm done my shift. I never miss Frontier Days. I don't think anyone does that's from around here."

Camilla's thoughts rushed quickly back to Beau.

"You go to all the places I suggested?"

"Yup, for sure. Got tons of great shots. Thanks so much for your help."

"No problem," she extended her hand. "I'm Lucy, by the way. If you need any more help with anything while you're here, just let me know back at the hotel."

They parted ways, and Camilla found that her buoyant mood had returned. How could it not, she mused? Everyone here was so friendly. She couldn't help but have a great time. Once she got her mind back onto business, she found lots of other people and things to photograph. Near the edge of the square, a small crowd had gathered to watch a tiny Papillon doing tricks and jumping through tiny hoops for his owner. It was an impromptu show, nothing on the itinerary, but great fun, none-theless. The little black and white dog was so adorable that she took numerous shots of it in action and afterward, in his owner's arms.

As she looked around, she realized for the first time, how many of the people in the crowd had actually brought their dogs with them. Most of the dogs wore colorful bandanas around their necks, and some of them sported cowboy hats and even sunglasses. Spotting a really old-looking Labrador Retriever, Camilla rushed over to ask its owner the dog's age. Fifteen, she smiled proudly, telling her she'd rescued him when he was just a puppy, about six weeks old. She was happy to pose for pictures and Camilla gave her one of her business cards to contact her later to get copies of some of the shots.

A middle-aged man in the crowd stopped her as she was walking away. He was a talent agent, he said, for models, actors, dancers, and even a few photographers.

"I noticed you taking a lot of pictures and I thought, if you ever want to do so professionally, you may want to give me a call."

Camilla laughed. She handed him one of her business cards out of her camera bag.

"Oh, I see you're way ahead of me, young lady. Well, congratulations! But what brings you all the way here to Frontier Days?"

She explained her assignment for Geographic Insight Magazine to document life in the Great Plains. The man nodded cheerfully, and they chatted for a little bit, discussing the freelance photography business as well as the festival they were at. He was more than helpful, suggesting other places she could go to get fantastic pictures if she had the time before she left. Watching him walk away, Camilla was enveloped by sudden nostalgia, remembering when photography was still a hobby to her, and a career in it was still a pipe dream. I'm so incredibly lucky, she thought, to be doing what I love and making a great living at it. Just as her smile reached the corners of her lips, Ann's voice echoed in her head. You need me to remind you to keep thinking about more than just your job. Just great, now she was thinking of Beau again.

She shrugged it off and continued meandering through the crowd. Soon, she was occupied with lots of new subjects for her photos. On the other side of the square, a gymnastics club was putting on a small show. The performers were dressed in gymnastic suits patterned with horses and cowboy hats and looked to be between the ages of eight to fourteen or fifteen. The music they performed to was, of course, a medley of country hits. Wow. Camilla couldn't believe how people here tied absolutely everything they did into their down-home western lifestyle. It got more interesting as she continued walking around. She noticed a mechanical bull had been set up and the lineup to ride it was long. Hope none of the people have been drinking, she smirked, as she focused her camera for a few shots. She'd just turned to walk away when she literally bumped into a clown dressed like a cowboy of course.

"No way!" she burst out laughing. "Even you're dressed like a cowboy," she smiled.

"Of course," he laughed. "Except for all the makeup and red nose, this is usually the way I dress."

She laughed so hard she nearly dropped her camera. He was more than happy to pose for pictures when she told him what they were for. She soon forgot about Beau as she found more and more interesting people to photograph. Until she saw a happy couple hugging tightly. By the looks of it, he'd just told her he loved her, maybe even proposed. With Beau inside her head once more, she wondered if she was ever going to find him and, more importantly, if the man she'd seen was really him or just someone with a close resemblance. Suddenly, she felt utterly foolish for maybe chasing someone who wasn't even here. She forced herself to get back to work but with her job garnering her attention, the discomforting thought nagged at her. Her work was keeping her from moving forward and actually someone; finding Beau if, in fact, he was around. If he is, I'll never find him now, she feared.

Not too long afterward, she ran into a man on stilts. Naturally, he was dressed as a cowboy as well. She snapped a bunch of pictures and thanked him, soon getting into a conversation about the skills required to navigate the world on stilts and not fall flat on your face and break some limbs. Casually glancing behind him at the people milling by, Camilla gasped. Beau. For sure, it was him. Relief flooded over her until she noticed the woman he was with, holding onto his hand. Damn. Her joy plummeted into despair. Unbeknownst to her, the blonde woman he was with was the very last person he wanted to be around. It was Carolyn. She'd run into him when he'd left setting up on stage to go and grab a cold beer for him and Greg. Quickly saying goodbye to the man on stilts, Camilla hesitated a second, taking a deep breath. Jealously washed over her as she stomped forward to go and confront him. Until she stopped in her tracks. What the hell? Am I going crazy, she winced. I have nothing to confront him about. I just met him, and he was kind enough to help me order at the diner, fix my flat tire, and pose for photos for my assignment. If there's anything between us, it's just in my own head.

Despite her remaining discomposure, and when she admitted it to herself – pain, she laughed it off as best she could, turned on her heels, and walked briskly in the other direction to get as far away from him as she could. For some reason, she just knew she'd feel incredibly uncomfortable if he spotted her while he was with his girlfriend. Or wife? She'd feel so stupid and even more embarrassed for flirting and for so obviously having a crush on him; someone she'd only just met. Anxious to put it all behind her, she grabbed the arm of almost the first person she saw when she reached the other end of the square.

"Hi, I'm Camilla Santos, a freelance photographer on assignment for Geographic Insight Magazine. I'm documenting Frontier Days and the people here. Would you mind letting me take some pictures of you?"

"Me? Um, sure. Why not? What do you want me to do?"

Even before the middle-aged woman agreed to the shoot, Camilla realized her mistake. There really was nothing exceptional about the woman. She'd just desperately wanted to start doing something to get her mind off Beau. But obviously, she had no desire to be rude and to tell the woman she'd changed her mind, so she went along with her own request. By the time she had her move from this pose into that one and then another, she acknowledged that the woman's photos wouldn't be so bad after all. Thanking her, she walked away, still deep in thought. This is crazy, she told herself. You don't even know what you're doing. Forget the guy who didn't like you anyway and get back to your job. Her resolve worked for a little bit, and she snapped about fifty or so new photos of people smiling and chatting and even of a cotton candy vendor handing out his offerings to children squealing in delight.

Good. She was proud of herself for not obsessing anymore about Beau. She was so done with that. About to grab her cell to update Ann, she decided against that too. Updating her would still be talking about Beau and he wasn't important enough to deserve a whole separate conversation dedicated to him. Strolling through the crowd, looking for more photo subjects, she moved to the edge of the square and out onto the street. Walking past Corner Coffee, a large two-floor café with a wraparound veranda on the second floor, she thought about taking a break and going inside for something to drink and to rest. Checking it out, she eyed their veranda and noticed Beau and the woman again. Damn.

She wanted to look away but just couldn't. It seemed they had just arrived upstairs on the veranda and were taking a seat together at a small round table. The woman couldn't be happier, Camilla cringed. I should have known. I shouldn't have just assumed he was single. My bad. My really bad this time. Just a split second before she forced herself to turn away, Beau glanced down at the street below him – and caught her eye.

Nine

STARTLED TO SEE CAMILLA, Beau was about to raise his hand and wave to her when she walked away. What the hell? he thought. He was sure that he had caught her eye. Resisting the urge to abandon Carolyn blabbering at their table, he forced himself to remain seated and turned back to look at her as she rambled on. So much for getting back to Greg quickly with our cold beers. Beau wondered why, yet again, he had allowed Carolyn to corner him. He concluded that he was just too damn nice for his own good. He should have simply told her he was too busy to go for coffee. Has she even gotten to the point yet? he mused, realizing he'd literally missed all of what she said.

"Sorry, what?" he forced a gracious smile. "I was going over the setlist in my head and didn't hear everything you said."

He had heard nothing of what she'd said. But it would have been too rude to admit that, despite his new inner resolve to stop being so damn nice. But, no problem, he cringed. He was sure Carolyn was simply going to start again from the beginning. She'd say anything to keep him with her longer and to glue him in place.

"Like I said, Beau," she gave him one of her best warm, flirtatious smiles, "I wanted to talk to you privately about this. I thought we might as well have some coffee as we..."

"Carolyn," he blurted, unable to stand it anymore. "I really don't have much time. Why don't you just tell me whatever you have to say?"

Instantly, her coy expression transformed into an exaggerated pout. Just lovely, Beau groaned, using all his effort not to wince. Maybe other men, although for the life of him he couldn't imagine who, found Carolyn's displays of overt affection, mixed with silly childishness, endearing. But he wasn't one of them, not by a long shot. Never in high school, he remembered, and certainly not now.

"I still have to finish setting up," he tried to ease the blow. "Remember, I pretty much put this gig together at the last minute just for you."

That did it. She mentally check-marked a point in her favor as he cringed. He could literally see the unabashed look of triumph flow over her fervid face. Damn, he thought. Maybe this wasn't the way to go.

"What can I get ya?" a smiling waitress appeared out of nowhere, forcing them from their thoughts.

Beau supposed he had to order. There was no way around staying here with Carolyn for at least a little bit.

"Just a regular coffee for me, thanks," he muttered, looking pointedly at Carolyn.

Just like he knew she would, she ordered something a little more complicated, something with flair.

"I'll have a pumpkin spice chocolate almond espresso with a double shot of whipped cream, and let's see...maybe a tiny sliver of that fantastic apple crumble dessert you have."

"Sure thing," their server nodded. "I'll be right back."

Not quickly enough, Beau snickered inside his head. The faster she brought their order, the faster he could gulp down at least some of his coffee and leave.

"So, what's up, Carolyn?"

He was surprised his voice had come out so even and calm when all he really wanted to do was scream.

"Well," she leaned across the table as he leaned away from her, as far back in his chair as he could. "I forgot to mention it earlier, but Jordy Evans is arriving shortly. He'll be one of the emcees tonight."

When Beau stared at her blankly, she continued, obviously flustered that her revelation had absolutely no effect.

"Surely, you've heard of him," she gushed. "I specifically invited him here for your benefit. He's one of the biggest record producers in Denver!"

Rather than eliciting the desired effect, Carolyn's news hit Beau like an unwelcome ton of bricks. Just peachy, he thought, like he wasn't already uncomfortable singing and playing in public. And like Greg wouldn't be all over him to book more gigs and pursue a recording contract if this Jordy guy was even the slightest bit impressed with their set. In utter shock for a moment, it took Beau a few seconds to respond. By the time he managed to stammer something that didn't sound as irritated as he felt, she'd literally half-crawled up onto their table, pulling his arm forward to grasp his hand.

"Carolyn, while I undoubtedly appreciate your effort, you know I have absolutely no plans to pursue any sort of music career in the least. My ranch takes..."

"But Greg will be so thrilled," she gushed, satisfaction and delight oozing from her voice.

He shrugged. Low blow, Carolyn, you desperate shrew, forcing him between a rock and a hard place, yet again. In fact, he realized, almost every single time that Carolyn opened her mouth to say anything, throughout all the years he'd known her, she'd only succeeded in turning him off, not on, as she intended. He yanked his hand out of her tight grasp.

"Greg knows how I feel about expanding our efforts with the band," he said as calmly as he could. "Even though he'd love to play a little more than we do, he runs his own ranch, not to mention Christie and his kids take precedence."

"Beau!" Carolyn slammed her hand down on the table, like a toddler about to have a temper tantrum for not getting her way. "You're just so talented! Why don't you realize it? Honestly, if you'd just work a little harder at advancing your music career, I swear you'd take off! Then you wouldn't have to bust your ass working so hard on your ranch."

He flinched. For someone who professed to be so crazy about him, she didn't know him in the least.

"My ranch is my life, Carolyn. Not because it has to be. Not because

I have no other choice. Because I love it and wouldn't, not even for a second, dream of doing anything else."

Beau's eyes were so turbulent, so focused and intense that for perhaps the first time in her life, she leaned away from him, speechless. But only for a second or two. Women like her always recover quickly. They always have a quick comeback and other ideas or approaches within their bag of tricks.

"I know this, Beau," she lied, nearly convincingly. "It's because you love your ranch so much that I thought you'd be thrilled at not having to work so hard on it every day. With the money and recognition of a record contract, you could take more time to simply enjoy your life on the ranch without having so much to do."

"I enjoy having lots to do on the ranch," he countered. "You're missing the point."

She pouted again, wishing that it would do her some good this time.

"Your espresso and apple crumble," their waitress hovered over their table unexpectedly. "And your coffee," she smiled. "Will that be all for now?"

Beau chimed in before Carolyn could say a word.

"That'll be it, thanks. We're in a little bit of a hurry. So, if you don't mind, we'd love our check."

"No problem. I'll be back in a sec."

"Beau, I was just trying to help you. I sure hope you haven't taken anything I've done the wrong way."

It was apparent she was telling the truth. Beau knew the last thing that Carolyn wanted was upset or alienate him.

"Don't worry about it," he grunted, taking a sip of his coffee. Then, he suddenly remembered a much more pleasant exchange when he stopped for a drink and some takeout food the other day.

At Deno's, and his chance meeting with Camilla. Damn, he glanced down at the street again, unnerved that she'd quickly wandered off and disappeared into the crowd. He was sure he'd caught her eye. She may be a little bit different, he mused, but it was all in a very endearing and pleasant way. He was thinking about how obvious it was that both Camilla and Carolyn liked him and how incredibly different they were. He thought about how Carolyn was attractive but pushy, manipulative, and domineering and how Camilla was even more attractive because she didn't even try to be. He thought about how flustered Camilla was at her own inadvertent displays of obvious attraction and how much that had very sweetly embarrassed her. Super handsome, he smiled cheerfully, recalling what she'd called him. He really needed to get out of the café and find her again.

"...so maybe that should be your last song in the set."

Carolyn's voice jolted him back to his current miserable reality.

"I'm sorry, what?"

She sighed, disheartened that she managed to lose his attention once again.

"I was just thinking, instead of Whiskey Blues, maybe Goodbye Mountain Rain ought to be your last song of the set."

"You were thinking, were you?" he quipped, this time not giving a damn about the irritation in his voice.

She just couldn't help herself from sticking her nose into his business, as if she had to have a hand in everything. He thought he'd successfully discouraged her from this topic, but apparently, he'd been wrong.

"Yes, well, when I think of each song's overall meaning and the final reaction you'd like to get from the crowd..."

"I think Greg and I are the best judges of the meaning of our songs. And," he leaned forward, fighting to keep the anger out of his voice, "we're pretty savvy to how our audiences react to each of those songs."

"Oh, of course. I only meant..."

"Is there anything else?"

"What? What do you mean?" she was taken aback.

"Anything else you needed to discuss with me. I really have to get back to Greg and finish setting up the stage."

"Right," she forced a smile. "No, not really. Not right now, anyway."

"Good," Beau snatched his half-empty coffee cup off the table and gulped the rest back.

He pushed back his chair to stand.

"Except..." she blurted.

He grunted and sank back into his chair. He swore it was as if Carolyn was some sort of venomous spider that tossed out invisible tentacles whenever her prey relaxed around her, especially if her victim was about to escape. Suddenly, he felt like he was lurching through quicksand, floundering to make his way back down to the freedom of the street, but he just couldn't take long or deep enough steps. How will I ever find or even catch up with Camilla, he suddenly thought, if I can't even make my way back to my own brother. And I know exactly where he is! He stared at Carolyn impatiently, waiting for her inevitable assertion or whatever she had to say to keep him sitting solidly in place.

"You know how you always bring up a girl from the audience during Two in Love to dance with you a little and sing to? Well, sometimes I've noticed that the girls you get up there are a bit shy or boring. I was thinking, I could pose like just someone in the crowd, and you could invite me up. I can add a bit of excitement..."

"No!"

Holy Christ, was she ever, ever going to give this shit up? Looking as hurt and pained as Beau expected her to, Carolyn crumpled back into her chair. Why on earth did she even think I'd allow this, he wondered. How can she possibly be so ignorant and unaware of how I've done literally almost everything possible to avoid close contact with her? I have never led her on even in the slightest throughout all these years. A grim cloud of silence loomed over them for a few moments until Carolyn regained her composure. Well, of course. It certainly wasn't like her to give up so easily or to give up at all.

"Fine, Beau. I know how you never want to admit when you need help."

Need help?! This time, it took Beau every ounce of determination and self-control he had not to blow his top. She was either not half as bright as he'd always thought or simply delusional. It didn't matter which. All he wanted was to get the hell away from her. He quietly stood. Forever a gentleman, he resisted the overwhelming urge to exit with a caustic jab. Reaching into the back pocket of his jeans, he pulled out his wallet and placed forty dollars on the table. Their server hadn't returned yet with their check.

"This should cover it, including the tip," he smiled. "Enjoy your dessert."

He eyed the closest exit and cringed. Beverly Teel, a local television reporter, was making her way with her camera crew toward them. Just great. He'd dated Beverly for a short time way back in high school, and it was no secret to anyone that she still had a thing for him. It was bad enough that she'd probably air some footage of him singing on the news tonight – he just knew she would – but the last thing he wanted was to give an interview. He glanced at the other exit, but it was too late. Smiling and making a fuss, she arrived at his table before he could make his great escape.

"Beau! Just the man I wanted to see," she stepped forward enthusiastically and placed her hand on his shoulder. "Long time no see."

He sighed.

"How are you, Bev? It's wonderful seeing you too, but I have to get back to the stage."

"You're not going on yet, are you?" she raised an eyebrow. "It's still a while before the show starts, right?"

"Right," he nodded, "but I have to finish setting up."

"This'll just take a few minutes, I promise," she broke out in the same warm smile she used every evening for the news. "I'd just like to get a few comments from you about..."

"Talk to Carolyn," he smirked, knowing Carolyn would jump at the chance to be on camera, allowing him the opportunity to get away.

"Well, you're who I..."

"Fantastic!" Carolyn pushed back her chair and stood.

Snickering, Beau quickly nodded to the two women, who he knew disliked each other, and strolled through the crowd quickly, slipping out the closest exit.

Ten

FUMING and shaking with rage and jealousy, Camilla pushed her way through the crowd as inconspicuously and politely as possible, away from Corner Coffee and quickly out of sight of Beau's view. He'd looked right at her, she was a thousand percent sure of it, and for some weird reason, she couldn't shake her resulting embarrassment. Embarrassed at what, she asked herself as she kept walking, weaving aimlessly through the laughing and joking people having the time of their lives. I have nothing to be embarrassed about, nothing at all. And certainly nothing to be jealous or angry about. But I am.

Thinking for a second that she'd just distract herself again by taking more photos, she decided against it this time. She was just too upset. Face it, girl. As unlikely as it is to go anywhere, you really have a major crush on this guy. She needed a drink. One huge plastic cup of beer. Although she rarely drank anything alcoholic while working on assignment, she decided this situation called for an abrupt change of rules. One beer wouldn't get her drunk, but it just might succeed in taking the edge off and relaxing her frazzled nerves. The musicians were due to start in about an hour, and she had to pull herself together before then if she was going to get some amazing shots.

Camilla was looking around for a booth selling alcohol when she was startled by her ringing phone. Fishing it out quickly from her camera bag, she sighed. Ann. There was something to be said for her best friend's timing. Sometimes, like now, it was spot on.

"My life sucks!" she said as she answered and started talking before Ann could say anything.

"Oh no! What now? More flying drinks? I thought you were walking today. You can't possibly have another flat tire."

"Nope. It's worse than that," Camilla groaned as she finally spotted the bright blue and red umbrella of a beer vendor.

She walked toward it, pushing her way through the crowd as fast as she could.

"Put it this way," she continued. "I've made an absolute ass of myself with Mr. So-called Super-Handsome, yet again."

"Ooh," Ann snickered. "This doesn't sound good. He's gone from Super Handsome to So-called Super Handsome. What the heck happened now?"

"Hang on. I'll tell you in a moment. I'm up next in line to grab a beer."

"You're done shooting already?"

"No. I still have to take photos of the main event, the three bands that'll start playing in about an hour. I just need a drink."

Ann waited patiently, listening quietly on the other end of the phone while Camilla asked for a large Budweiser. Whatever happened, she thought, it must be a doozy. Camilla was anything but a drinker, even when they went out to clubs. Camilla rarely had more than one or two beers throughout the entire evening, even when they were partying. And she was the least likely of her friends to suck back booze while still on the job. The talking and laughing background noise faded as Camilla made her way to a much quieter area where she could talk.

"Okay. I'm off in a little mini-park thing at the far end of the square. Looks like most of the people that were hanging out here have already made their way up to the stage."

Hearing a slight grunt and sigh, Ann determined that Camilla had sat herself down.

"You're sitting on the grass, aren't you?" she asked, instinctively knowing this is what Camilla would do if she truly lost it for whatever reason during a job.

"Yeah, I'm just so mad I needed to take a seat and chill."

"So? Tell me what happened. You have some sort of argument or something with this guy Beau?"

"Not even close. And there's absolutely no way I'm ever going to even speak to him again now."

"Huh? This is your first beer, right? Camilla, either I missed something major in our conversation, or you're not exactly making a whole lot of sense. What are you skipping over? Why are you so angry? What did he do?"

Taking a long sip of her beer, Camilla groaned. And realized that Beau hadn't actually done anything. Her embarrassment, jealousy, and anger were totally misplaced. Beau was simply going about his business, his usual life, and it obviously didn't include her. But why should it? They barely knew each other and certainly hadn't established a relationship of any kind. Loose friendship, maybe. But certainly not a romantic one.

"Damn, Ann. He really didn't do anything," she admitted when the stark realization hit her. "It's just that I realized my romantic connection with him is all in my head."

"Realized, how? You run into him again?"

"Not exactly."

"Then..."

"I saw him. He was walking hand-in-hand with some real hotsy-totsy blonde babe. He didn't see me, then. Just a few minutes ago, I spotted him at this coffee house, up on the veranda, taking a seat with her. He looked down on the street and saw me this time."

"Okay..." Ann's tone was expectant.

She was waiting for the punchline, the climax of this little event.

"It's not okay!" Camilla blurted. "He looked right at me, and I feel sooo, sooo stupid! Here I am thinking about him, searching for him for Christ's sake, and he's off gallivanting around with this, this...strumpet the whole entire time."

Ann couldn't help herself. She burst out laughing. Who the hell even used words like strumpet anymore?

"Oh, God, Camilla. I'm sorry," she mumbled, still unable to contain her laughter. "I apologize girlfriend. I know you're upset. It's just the way you're talking. Strumpet, really? Are we back in the Victorian age or something? Has Beau disgraced you by toying with your heart and emotions before running off with the woman in red?"

"Very funny!" Camilla jeered but did manage to see the humor, despite her pain.

"You know, you could have just gone up and talked to him. I mean, to at least find out who the chick was before getting your panties all in a knot."

"It's obvious!" Camilla moaned. "He sure as hell wasn't holding hands with his sister, that's for sure."

"You got a point. But really, did you at least wave to him or something to gauge the look on his face?"

"No."

"The look on a guy's face is really telling when you see him and he's with another woman. If he's shocked and startled to see you, you know he knows he's been caught. If he's happy to see you show up, then the other girl means nothing or very little to him."

"Well, yeah, I guess, but..."

"So, okay, you didn't wave to him or anything when you guys saw each other but what was his expression like? Surprised? Happy? Guilty? What???"

"Oh crap, I don't know Ann. I just looked away quickly and got the hell out of there."

Silence weighed heavily between them until a few seconds later. After some thought, Ann spoke again.

"Here's what you do. There's absolutely no point in you pining over this guy when you're not even sure what his situation is. Go back there. Try and find him. Heck, you guys already know each other. Just say hi and talk to him."

"I...I just can't," Camilla's voice broke with emotion.

At a loss for words again for a few moments, Ann's voice softened as she cut to the chase.

"Camilla, why are you so hurt?"

Ann's acknowledgment of her feelings embellished them for some

70

reason, and Camilla winced at the actual pain of grief and betrayal in her chest. This is stupid, she thought. Beau is someone I just met. Simply a nice, friendly guy and nothing more.

"I can't really explain it. I guess I just really like him. A lot."

"Happens to the best of us," Ann sympathized. "But before you totally give up on this one, at least make sure you're not bowing out before the final curtain. You're jumpin' off the stage, girlfriend, as the plot thickens because you're so afraid the plot's climax won't turn out so well."

This, finally, elicited a giggle from Camilla. Leave it to Ann to find a way to cheer her up in the middle of this mess.

"Ever thought of becoming a therapist?" Camilla asked her, still laughing.

"Nooo way," Ann snickered. "Not when I'm only good at giving advice but not taking it and using it for myself. I think therapists are supposed to be much more put together than I am, with perfect lives, perfect husbands or boyfriends, a great house, white picket fence, and all that and 2.5 kids."

"Stop it!" Camilla laughed. "There's nothing wrong with your life. I'm the one who abandoned my usually perfect dedication to the job and professionalism to fall apart at the first cowboy she met with a chiseled jaw and gorgeous eyes."

"I see," Ann snickered, "So Beau's gone from Mr. So-called Super Handsome back to Mr. Super Handsome again?"

"Yeah," Camilla sighed. "But that doesn't mean I'm going to go chasing after him again. Not by a long shot in hell. No matter how I look at it, he was much too nice to me. Much too smooth for a guy who's already attached."

"But how firmly?"

Damn it, Ann, Camilla flinched. Her friend wasn't about to let her just give up.

"Firmly enough, by the looks of it. Even though I don't really have a right to be mad..."

Ann saw that Camilla was still vacillating.

"...I do have the right to be at least more than a little annoyed. I'm telling you, he was way too friendly. Way too, I don't know, way too seemingly single. But I have no inkling to make an ass of myself in front of him again."

"Okay."

"Okay?"

"Sure it is. If you don't really want to know what could have happened; if you'd swallowed your fears to find out if this casual friendship could actually lead to anything more."

"If he were single," Camilla asserted.

"Key word is if," Ann shot back. "Look, if Beau's attached – steady girlfriend, fiancé, wife, whatever – then you'll have your answer. If he's not, you'll get a good idea by how he reacts to you and whether you two can go anywhere from here."

"Yeah, right. And..."

"And all you have to risk is a broken heart. Which, by the way, is already broken at the moment anyway, so seriously, what have you really got to lose?"

"Nothing," Camilla said while silently thinking, my self-esteem and dignity, until she realized she was so much better than that. "I'm not defined by what some random guy, no matter how charming and good-looking, thinks of me. I've never been, and I'm certainly not going to start now. I have a great career, no shortage of great boyfriend prospects, and...and I don't need a man in my life, whether or not I decide I may want one!"

"You go girl!"

Downing the last of her beer, Camilla stood.

"Enough of this crap!" her self-help pep talk continued. "I'm going back there to find this guy and talk to him. No matter who he's with."

"Keep me posted...."

"Yup."

Camilla had barely taken a few steps forward after hanging up her phone and shoving it back into her camera bag when her resolve weakened. Not a lot, but a little. Damn it. That blonde lady Beau was with was so attractive, she remembered. And they were holding hands. Still, she straightened as she pushed herself forward. I have every right in the world to talk to him, to say hello again. I have absolutely nothing to be so damn afraid of. No reason at all to be mad at him. She kept that attitude rigid and firmly implanted until she emerged on the street below Corner Coffee and looked back up onto the veranda. Beau was now up there at the table with not one but two women. The long-haired brunette was gushing all over him with her hand caressing his shoulder. Damn!

All of Camilla's resolve to remain aloof and indifferent, casually friendly and nonconfrontational, flew out the window as her jealousy and blood boiled. Apparently, she huffed, I've totally misjudged him. His seemingly innocent, down-home politeness and charm were nothing more than a slick façade to draw in and capture more women. Beau's a player, she decided, and screw him if he thought for just one second that I'd play his game. Seething with anger and frustration at how easily he'd roped her in, she stared up at him on the veranda, silently daring him to look down again and meet her eyes. But of course he didn't. No surprise, she told herself bitterly. He's much too busy raking in the compliments and whatever else the women were throwing his way.

Watching as they gushed and fawned all over him, Camilla wondered just how comfy and complacent they'd feel when they realized he had at least one other girl waiting in the wings. Me. If he even considers me eligible and worthwhile. When that peachy thought hit her, she was toast. Stop it! It makes no difference whatever this roving, wayward cowboy thinks. Even so, she straightened her shoulders again, I have a good mind to march right up there and disrupt his little gathering, making it clear that all I ever wanted was some casual friendship if I even wanted that much at all. I'll teach him a lesson, she thought as she stomped across the street to the café. He might think we all want to be part of his little harem, but I'll show him that not every woman is stupid enough to fall for that. Certainly not me.

She was surprised at how busy and packed the place was when she stepped inside. Well, of course. What am I thinking? It's obviously busier than normal because of Frontier Days. There was a long and winding double lineup for seating, but she thought nothing at all of bypassing it. She had no intention of sitting down at Beau's table or anywhere else under the circumstances. She had absolutely no plans to stay.

73

"Excuse me, miss?" she spun around toward the voice behind her. "I'm sorry, but we're super busy at the moment and I'm afraid that you'll have to take your place at the end of the line."

Seriously? She forced a smile even as she felt her face flushing crimson with anger and nervousness.

"Oh, that's okay. I'm not actually staying. I just have to run upstairs quickly and tell my friend something before I leave."

The server looked at her disbelievingly for a second. His face darkened, then smoothed as he decided to take her at her word.

"Sure, go ahead. No problem."

Her heart pounded in her chest. Camilla rushed down the aisle, past the packed tables with joking and laughing patrons, and bounded up the stairs to the veranda. If Beau thinks for even a second...Her jaw dropped as she stared at his table. And for the first time, she noticed the brunette's camera crew filming behind her as she interviewed the chatty, animated blonde. But they were alone. Beau had darted out another exit just before she got there and was gone.

Eleven

"TWO LARGE BUSCH, PLEASE."

Standing at the same vendor that Camilla had recently visited, Beau was finally grabbing the beers for Greg and himself. He winced. No doubt his brother would ask him what had taken him so long to get back, and he'd have to admit that, yet again, he'd caved into one of Carolyn's ridiculous schemes to get some alone time with him. Nothing she'd had to say to him had to be spoken in private. It had just been another bid to garner more of his attention and win his affection and gratitude in some way.

Wondering if he should even tell his brother about Carolyn inviting Jordy Evans, the record producer, to their performance tonight, Beau felt guilty for even considering keeping it from him. Greg would be thrilled, probably even a little nervous, and Beau knew he'd now have to deal with his brother's wanting to expand their very part-time musical career. Damn Carolyn, she just doesn't know when to quit.

"Here you go," the vendor handed him two large plastic cups of beer.

Making his way back to the stage through the milling crowd without spilling any of it was more difficult than he'd planned. Everyone around him seemed so excited about the band starting up soon and

Frontier Days in general that they paid little attention to what they were doing and who was around them. Wouldn't it be just great, Beau grimaced, if someone makes me spill this all over myself? He hadn't brought any extra clothing and was already dressed for the stage. Well, if one of his best pairs of jeans and plaid shirts counted as dressing up. Beau liked to keep it casual and laid-back, like playing was no big deal.

It's a miracle, he mumbled to himself as he rounded the side of the stage and mounted the steps. Greg was chatting with Matt, and by the looks of it, they were pretty well finished setting up. Matt spotted him before Greg and smiled, joking with him as he approached.

"We thought you'd gone AWOL on us, buddy. Or gotten kidnapped," he laughed.

"Kidnapped is a nice way to put it," Beau grumbled, handing Greg his beer. "Sorry, didn't get you one, Matt. I can run back if you want."

His friend shook his head, "No need. I just finished one."

"So, where were you? What took you so long?" Greg asked.

"One guess," Beau smirked.

"Carolyn!" Greg and Matt blurted at the same time.

"Maybe we ought to assign you a bodyguard or something, Beau. Do you think?" Greg was still laughing.

"What I'm starting to think," Beau snickered, "is that kidnapping isn't such a bad idea."

His brother and friend stared at him in disbelief.

"I mean getting her kidnapped and taken far, far away from here."

With that, they all burst out laughing once again. After Matt went off to finish preparations, Beau and Greg completed everything else they had to do on their end.

"What do you say we go relax a bit? There's still a little bit of time before we go on."

"Sure, what are you thinking?"

"Just in the performers' tent behind the stage. I bet Mom and everyone are already there waiting for us. You know she doesn't feel right if she doesn't wish us good luck before we go on."

"Yeah, right. Okay."

It had become sort of a family tradition for everyone to gather before Beau and Greg's band performed. As irritated as he was with

Carolyn, Beau tried hard to shake off his bad mood. No way was he going to let her ruin this night for him when he should be having fun. His thoughts drifted back to Camilla. How would he ever find her now that he was out of time to look?

"You guys look great!" Ellie said as she spotted and approached her sons to give them both a huge hug.

"Well Mom, we all know you have to say that. We're your kids," Greg laughed.

"I know," she laughed. "But I really mean it, boys. You're looking pretty dapper tonight." Eyeing Beau as she continued, she raised an eyebrow inquisitively. "You bring a date tonight?"

"Here we go," Greg snickered, bursting out laughing as he walked away. "I'll just leave you in Mom's clutches, bro, and you can fend for yourself!"

"Thanks, I owe you one now!" Beau joked with him before turning back to his mom.

"Nope. No date. Just on my lonesome for this evening."

"Again?"

"Yes, Mom. Again," he leaned down and kissed her cheek. "Unless you want to hook me up with Carolyn. Try as I might to get away, she's been pretty well glued to my side since I got here."

"Oh, Lordy!" Ellie laughed. "I'm not that desperate to get you hitched!"

She'd watched Carolyn chase her son all through his high school years and had been about as relieved as he'd been when she finally got engaged to someone else. No one was surprised, though, when she set her sights back on Beau after her divorce.

"What's that covetous woman done now?" Ellie laughed.

Beau filled her in about the record producer from Denver and Carolyn's attempted meddling with his song list. Ellie was shaking her head throughout Beau's tirade and accidentally spat her lemonade out, laughing hysterically when Beau told her how she'd suggested that he invite her up on stage for him to sing to during one of his songs.

"Well, that's all you need," she patted his back lovingly, "is to encourage her in any way at all."

"Exactly! That's why I couldn't say no quickly enough."

Their conversation was interrupted when a bright pink balloon landed on Ellie's lap. Lacy, her youngest granddaughter, ran up and grabbed it. She and her little brother were swatting it through the air in their own version of volleyball.

"Careful you don't hit it too hard, Lacy," Beau warned, "or it'll pop."

"I know!" the little girl laughed. "Me and Tucker already popped a few."

While watching his niece and nephew playing for a few minutes, Beau's cheek suddenly burned with the feel of his mother's eyes on him.

"What?"

"I'm just hoping your brother Jayce isn't the last of my sons to give me some grandchildren," she smirked.

"Mom! Honestly, do you ever think of much else?"

"Not often," she laughed.

This type of friendly exchange between them had become the norm, especially over the last few years as Beau got a little older. Ellie worried about him not finding the love of his life. If it were anyone but his mother badgering him so much about it, Beau would have been royally pissed by now. But he knew she wanted only the best for him and that her intentions were all good, so he let it slide as much as he could.

"What did Greg say about that record producer being here tonight?" Ellie asked, thankfully changing the subject.

"Nothing yet. I actually forgot to tell him. Now Mom," he wagged his finger at her, "don't you even start sounding like him, encouraging us to work a little more toward having a real musical career."

"I wouldn't dream of it," she said. "My job is encouraging my boys to have large families with lots of kids," she laughed.

"Okay, I'm out of here," Beau joked as he stood and sauntered away to go and grab another drink before they hit the stage.

Seeing that Greg was sitting on a lawn chair beside Christie, Beau headed there. Christie got much more excited about the record producer than her husband, which surprised Beau a little. Maybe married life had mellowed Greg's personal ambitions more than Beau had realized. In any case, that was good because Beau's own plans didn't include striving to become a country music star.

"Greg was telling me about Carolyn," Christie said as Beau took a chair. "I honestly think you should invite her up on stage to sing to. It'd be hilarious!"

"No!" Beau burst out laughing. "We're not a comedy act."

"Ten minutes!" Matt strode by them, giving a heads-up about the show's impending start.

"Okay guys," Christie said, standing, "I'm going to round up the kids and try and find a good place to stand near the side of the stage where I can keep them reasonably quiet for a while."

"Good luck with that," Greg joked.

He knew his children were energetic, to say the least, but it was obvious that they meant the world to him.

"Ready, bro?" he eyed Beau as he stood from his chair.

"As I'll ever be," Beau laughed.

As much as he didn't want to pursue a music career, he had to admit that he really enjoyed himself when they played. His duties at the ranch kept him so busy that he never had much time to relax and have fun. Well, at least I enjoy my real career, Beau mused, thinking about how much work and effort he put into his cattle. As much effort as Camilla seems to put into her photography career, he thought, as his mind drifted back to her again. Is she still wandering around here somewhere? Surely, she'd be staying to get photos of the bands, the main event. For a moment, he wondered if there was enough time to stroll through the crowd and look for her. Obviously not. He leaped up from his chair, following Greg to stand at the side of the stage to await the emcee's introduction.

"You look way too deep in thought," Greg nailed him.

His brother always knew when something, in this case, someone, weighed heavily on his mind.

"Nah," he shrugged. "Not really. I was just thinking about how we dodged a bullet by not letting Carolyn come up on stage. There's no telling what kind of stunt she'd pull."

"Yup, that's for sure," Greg smirked before his expression turned more pensive again. "Something else on your mind? I can tell when you're distracted. It's not that record producer being here tonight, is it? I'm not even nervous, and I'm the one who sure wouldn't mind squeezing a record deal into my busy life."

Beau laughed at that. So, his brother's ambitions were still there, just boiling somewhat more quietly underneath the surface.

"Hell no," I forgot about him till you just mentioned it. "Believe it or not," he began before he could stop himself, "I was actually thinking about that photographer, Camilla. Wondering if she's still here in the crowd somewhere."

"Oh?" Greg looked surprised.

Beau had stopped himself from talking about her anymore to his brother because he didn't want to come off as hankering after a woman he'd just casually met and wasn't likely to hitch up with if he ever saw her again. He told Greg how he'd spotted her down on the street when he'd been sitting on the veranda at Corner Coffee and how she'd disappeared into the crowd.

"You sure that she saw you up there?"

"Seems like I caught her eye, yeah, but maybe not. She wandered away right afterward."

"Probably didn't see you then."

"Probably not."

Just as he agreed with Greg and said it, the thought hit Beau that maybe Camilla had seen everything, and clearly. He'd been sitting up there with Carolyn. And most of the time, when he hadn't succeeded in wrenching away, she'd been holding onto his hand. Just great. Now, the one woman he actually had an interest in probably thought he was involved with the one woman who was the last prospect on his list. He groaned.

"What?" Greg turned to him, confused.

"I was up there with Carolyn, remember? She was always holding onto my hand before I slid it away. And just before I managed to escape her clutches, Beverly showed up. She was all over me too."

"Right. You think that Camilla saw you up there and saw a little too much."

"Exactly."

Greg was surprised at how pained his brother looked.

"Look, this is all just conjecture. You know it's possible she didn't see you at all. By what you told me earlier about how she acted at the diner and when you changed her tire and stuff, she really liked you and didn't manage to hide it very well. I think she would have gone up there onto the veranda to talk to you if she had noticed you were there."

"Maybe..." Beau's voice trailed off in dejected reverie.

"In any case, she's here shooting Frontier Days, so she's likely to stick around for all of us bands. You might see her at the front of the stage."

"I'll be singing."

"Yeah, okay," Greg laughed. "That doesn't mean you can't smile and nod. We're not exactly Garth Brooks, you know. You can lean down and talk to her between songs."

That finally eased his mind and Beau began laughing too.

"If all else fails," Greg jabbed him in the ribs with his elbow, "you told me she gave you her business card, right? They've invented something called a telephone. We're actually using super convenient cell phones now."

"Very funny," Beau smirked.

But no matter how he looked at it, he was glad that his brother's usual great advice and cheerfulness had buoyed him up. It wouldn't do to hit the stage in a miserable mood. While this wasn't exactly his first public performance, he wasn't a seasoned star who was accustomed to hiding his inner thoughts and state of mind.

"So, you didn't stick around long enough to watch a fist fight between Carolyn and Beverly over you?"

"Hell no," Beau started laughing even harder than Greg. "I would have been pulled right smack dab into the middle of the skirmish somehow!"

"That I believe! But hey, look at the bright side. You don't have too much to complain about. What guy doesn't want two pretty women wanting him at the same time?"

Three women, Beau thought silently. Hoping it was actually three and that Camilla hadn't given up, that she hadn't stopped liking him somehow.

Twelve

~

WHERE THE HELL did he go? Still feeling incredibly conspicuous, Camilla glanced around at the entire veranda. Beau was nowhere in sight. Just wonderful. She'd spent all this time working up her resolve and courage to confront him, and now he was gone. To the men's room? she suddenly wondered. She doubted it. His chair was pushed back and his coffee cup looked empty and pushed to the center of the table. And the women didn't look like they were expecting him back. Apologizing and moving out of the way of the doorway as a patron squeezed by her, she stood a little longer and watched the blonde giving the brunette an interview. While flashing her best newscaster smile, the brunette asked another question, and the blonde droned on and on, oblivious to the eventual nods of the reporter signaling her to finish it up.

Well, whoever she is, whomever they both are, Camilla thought, still bristling with jealousy and tension as she looked at them, it really doesn't matter too much. What mattered was the fact that they obviously seemed to matter to Beau. Jesus, she winced, realizing she was still a victim of her pain and lengthy reasoning. Stop it, she thought. You came here to confront him, to get a feel of the situation, to see if he had any real feelings for you. Spying on these women and making conjectures isn't going to change anything. She moved closer to their table to see if she could overhear some of the interview anyway. The blonde must be someone important, Camilla guessed, or she wouldn't be making the evening news. It doesn't matter who she is; she was holding Beau's hand. She groaned and stepped closer again.

"And of course, because this year's entertainment is so fabulous, I've invited Jordy Evans, the well-known record producer from Denver, to be one of our emcees."

She invited him? Camilla huffed. She was probably one of the organizers of Frontier Days. Well, I'll be damned if I'm going to take her picture, she fumed. She spun and stomped back out the door and down the stairs. Time to get back to work, Camilla, she prodded herself. You have your own work to do here at the festival. Enough wasting time and worrying about anyone else, including Beau. With her resolve back to concentrate solely on her assignment, she exited the cafe quickly, crossed the street, and merged back into the crowd inside the square. Within minutes, pre-recorded music blared from the speakers on stage, warming up the audience for the first band slated to start performing soon. Good, she thought. Maybe watching some great entertainment would relax her and get her mind off Beau.

In the meantime, she decided to get some more shots. Lots of people in the crowd were dancing to the recorded music, adults and kids alike. Despite her remaining tension, she began picking up and incorporating the buoyant mood of the crowd. Thank God that Beau left before I got up there, she finally decided, relieved that she was averted before making a fool of herself in her angry mood. Once or twice, much more if she admitted it, she caught herself glancing around and searching the crowd for him. Nope, not going there, her inner voice chided her over and over again, to no avail.

"Excuse me, miss?" the tap on her arm jolted her from her reverie.

She'd been aiming her camera at a group of teens dancing near her and was startled at the unexpected interruption.

"Did you happen to see a small, elderly woman wandering around, looking kind of lost?"

"Uh, no," she replied, surprised at the question and the look of concern on the old man's face.

"Oh, okay. No problem. I just saw you were looking around, taking pictures, and hoped you'd noticed her somewhere."

Dejected, he turned to shuffle off.

"Wait a sec," her senses switched onto high alert. "Is there something wrong? Can I help in some way?"

"Well," he sighed, looking much older than his 78 years. "I'm looking for Mildred, my wife. I turned my back for a second and let go of her hand and she walked away. She has dementia and may not know where she is or even who she is if someone asks her."

"Oh, my goodness!" Camilla exclaimed. "Why don't I help you look for a few minutes? If we don't find her, I'm sure there's some sort of emergency announcement system, and we can get it announced so others will look for her too."

"Thank you!" his grateful smile tugged at her heart. "My name's Gerald, young lady. I can't thank you enough for being so kind."

"Don't mention it," she said, hooking her arm in his as they gently pushed their way through the increasingly boisterous crowd. "I'm Camilla. I'm here taking photos of Frontier Days for a magazine."

They chatted as they searched for Mildred. She shouldn't be that hard to find, Camilla noted to herself after Gerald had given her a description of his wife. How many extremely short little old ladies with grayish-blue hair could there possibly be wandering around and probably talking to themselves? At Camilla's urging, they checked out all the places in the square where Gerald hadn't searched yet and asked people whether they'd seen her anywhere.

"It's no use!" Gerald groaned in desperation just as Camilla stopped a young couple with two children and questioned them.

"I knew it!" the woman said, glaring at her husband. "Didn't I tell you, Mike, that things didn't look right?"

"Yeah," he nodded sheepishly.

"You saw her?" Gerald chimed in.

"I'm sure of it," the woman said, pointing to the other end of the square. "We saw an elderly, confused-looking woman talking to herself right near the statues. She was headed toward the park."

"Thank you so much!" Camilla patted her arm and pulled Gerald along with her as she turned to walk away.

"Oh, my," he winced. "I'm sorry. I'm walking too slowly. We're not going to catch up with her."

He was right. Gesturing for him to stay put, Camilla ran off in the direction where his wife was last seen. Constantly apologizing for bumping into people or ramming them with her camera bag, she scanned the crowd as she moved through it as fast as possible. Finally, not too far from the statues, she found a woman that could only be Mildred. Tiny and frightened looking, she was talking loudly to herself as she shuffled aimlessly. Camilla rushed to her side.

"Hi there, Mildred?"

The woman looked up blankly at her. Camilla remembered Gerald saying she might not know her own name.

"Gerald's looking for you," she told her gently. "Your husband."

Still the empty stare.

"Come on," Camilla grabbed her hand, tugging it lightly, encouraging her to follow along.

Luckily, she gave Camilla no problems as they walked back to her anxiously awaiting spouse. Gerald's face lit up as soon as he saw her. Rushing forward, he tightly embraced his wife.

"Young lady, Camilla, I can never thank you enough!"

"No problem. I'm just so happy I could help!"

Watching as Gerald gave Mildred a gentle scolding for scaring him half to death, Camilla breathed a huge sigh of relief. It was frightening how vulnerable the elderly were, especially when their physical or mental health was compromised. Musing about how she was looking at long-term true love and wondering how long they'd been married, she asked if she could take their picture. Life in The Great Plains moved at a much slower, more comfortable pace, and she just bet that the divorce rate here was much lower than in many other states.

"Why not?" Gerald laughed. "I'll hang this up and remember the day that Mildred almost got away from me."

He told her they'd been married for sixty years come next month as Camilla handed him her business card. They wandered off together, hand-in-hand, as Camilla smiled and watched. Hand-in-hand, she suddenly recalled. Beau had been walking hand-in-hand with the blonde. Ugh, here I go again, she flinched. You don't even know, she told herself, who the blonde is and what real importance, if any, she has in Beau's life. Still, as she sauntered back to the middle of the square, toward the stage, Camilla couldn't help wondering if the blonde was his wife. Beau did seem like the kind of guy that, once hooked, would stick around for the long haul. Maybe even sixty years.

Whatever. Move on, Camilla, she chided herself before stopping a large family to take their photos even though they weren't dancing like the rest of the crowd. As she looked around for other subjects, she listened to the announcement from the stage. The first act was coming on in ten minutes. Finally, she sighed. I can start to take the last of my photos here and get back to my hotel and relax. With any luck, all the bands would be enjoyable, or it would make for a very long night. How bad can they be, she wondered, as she snapped pictures of the excited crowd. They have to be somewhat good, or they wouldn't have been booked for such a major event. The hotel clerk had told her the live musical entertainment was the absolute highlight of Frontier Days.

"Do you work for KGWN?" a middle-aged woman stopped her as she made her way through the crowd snapping pictures.

"No. Is that the local news station?"

"Yup," the woman beamed. "My sons are in the band performing, and I was hoping to get some professional pics. My own camera sucks almost as bad as my photography skills!"

Camilla couldn't help laughing along with the proud mother. She could relate even though she had no kids of her own. Her own mom had been just as indulgent and supporting of her burgeoning career in photography long before Camilla knew she would make it a way of life.

"Tell you what," Camilla told her, "I'm here for Geographic Insight Magazine, but I sure don't mind taking some pictures of your sons and emailing them to you."

She fished out one of her business cards and asked the woman to write her name and email address on the back before she slid it back into her bag.

"And you never know," she told her cheerfully, "my editor may just choose one of the photos of your sons to be published in the magazine."

"Oh wow, I hope so!" the woman smiled almost literally from ear to ear.

"Who are they?" Camilla called out before the woman walked away, wanting to focus on the correct members of the band.

"One of them is the singer!" the woman fist-pumped the air as she made her way closer to the stage, too excited to finish her sentence, not wanting to miss a thing.

Hmm, the singer, Camilla smirked. She'd always had a thing for singers in bands. They always seemed to be the most handsome and talented ones. Realizing she was listening to the first strums of a guitar, she knew the first act was about to start. The crowd shifted and parted around her as people rushed forward, determined to be as close to the stage as they could. I'll get there, Camilla mused, and decided to take lots of photos of the crowd on her way to the front. Her efforts were rewarded as the crowd broke into applause while the singer launched into his first song. It was fantastic. Upbeat. Catchy. A true down-home country beat with a really unique sound. To her surprise, she found herself dancing, often just letting her camera hang down loosely from her neck. The dancing and waving crowd blocked her view of the stage, but it didn't matter. She wanted more shots of them enjoying themselves before she took any photos of the band.

Camilla literally swooned as the most mesmerizing rendition of Fields of Gold surrounded her. The singer's voice conjured visions of sunsets and farmer's fields that captured Camilla's heart, like a piece of her was bound to this place somehow.

As she danced and occasionally lifted her camera to take more pictures, she couldn't help thinking of Beau again. It was the lyrics. Country lyrics always made you think of long-lost, deep love. Yeah right, she shrugged her shoulders, trying to shrug off that thought. Love is for people you actually know well, she admitted to herself. In reality, she really didn't know Beau at all. But that sure doesn't mean I don't want to, she grudgingly acknowledged that sentiment too. It was getting harder and harder to focus on her assignment as her thoughts and feelings spun out of control. She wasn't used to that, making it all that much worse. Finally refocusing after she imagined herself trying to explain to her editor why her last photos had turned out like crap, she resigned herself to literally ignoring the sound of the music and focusing only on the actions and excitement of the crowd.

It helped that the audience was super responsive and photogenic. She got tons of pictures of women atop their boyfriend's or husband's shoulders, smiling and waving their hands in the air to the beat of the song. To get a better look, kids of all ages perched similarly on the shoulders of their dads. She grinned. Unlike rock and heavy metal, country music was so family-oriented. Even though some of the songs were sad, they always seemed to be filled with hope, and you just knew that things would somehow work out in the end. The band's first song ended with a boisterous round of applause. Whoever they are, Camilla thought, they're really good, extra well-known and popular, at least around here.

When their next number began, she noticed many people in the audience singing along. Spotting a little red-haired girl with pigtails sitting on her father's shoulders and waving, Camilla repositioned herself to get the best photos of her. The child's father turned to her quickly, looking concerned.

"Oh, don't worry!" Camilla smiled, quickly fishing a business card from her bag. "I'm here on assignment for Geographic Insight Magazine."

After they chatted for a few minutes, the little girl's dad thanked her for taking the photos and wished her the best of luck with the rest of her job. Camilla sighed as she walked away, inching closer to the stage. What was I thinking, she chided herself yet again. Normally she never, ever took photos of children, not even in a public place, without asking the parents or guardians for permission first. Doing her best to shake off her lapse in judgment, she pushed it to the back of her mind as she got caught up in the band's current song. This one was even better than the first. She couldn't help herself from continuing to dance in between grabbing more audience shots. Then, the song ended, and she got the shock of her life.

"Thanks so much, ladies and gentlemen. This next one's for all you single gals out there."

Oh. My. God. She knew that voice. It was her favorite cowboy, Beau. Lowering her camera, she sidestepped and circled, trying to get in front of people, doing everything she could to get to the front of the stage. It was no use. Beau's band was too popular, and the crowd wouldn't give way. Suddenly remembering she was carrying her camera equipment,

she loudly began announcing she was press, so the crowd parted wherever she shoved her way through. She literally gasped when she saw him
at the microphone, looking so confident and handsome. Strumming his
guitar, Beau launched into his next song just as Camilla arrived directly
below him at the front of the stage. He didn't miss a beat as their eyes
locked and he continued his song.

Thirteen

THE TUNES WERE PERFECT. Although Beau never liked being the center of attention, playing in the band was one of the best parts of his life. His bandmates were his friends and partners, and the music they made was enough to take him away from the stresses and strains of everyday life. The fact that the crowd was clearly into the sound only made it that much better.

Beau played to the crowd. They were moving to the music. But it wasn't exactly dancing. It was more like they were doing jumping jacks without using their arms. Still, the crowd was in tune with what he was singing, and Beau could "hide" in the sound. The crowd gazed at the band. But they were hypnotized by the songs and not paying attention to Beau, which helped him relax a bit. He gathered the music around him and reveled in the lyrics. They were playing an older tune, but one still popular; Beau and the rest of the band added some flourishes that weren't in the original.

Someone pushing through the crowd caught his eye, and he turned. The smile on his face faltered when he saw her and his heart skipped a beat. The beautiful klutz. Camilla. Here. Her camera was slung around her neck as she pushed through while yelling something. During an instrumental section where he didn't have to sing, he heard her yelling

"PRESS," and the crowd reluctantly parted. Maybe it was a reaction to her claims of being press. Or perhaps she was just so startling that people stopped to stare at her, and she took advantage of the moment.

Seeing her there threw Beau off-balance. For a moment, he forgot to breathe. His hands faltered on his guitar. It was a shock and confusing as his mind didn't process what he saw.

When the lyrics resumed, Beau came in late and repeated the words from the previous verse. No one seemed to notice, or perhaps they just didn't care. But his bandmates were looking at him as though they were worried. Everyone but the drummer was lost in his own world and saw nothing further away than his snare.

Beau looked away from her to the edge of the crowd. He looked at the flags in the distance, at anything that wasn't her. But his eyes kept returning like a moth to a flame. The phrase stuck in his head and repeated until he was at risk of singing that instead of the right words. If they had fit the tune, he probably would have.

She was directly at his feet now, staring up at the stage. He couldn't determine the look she was giving him. Was it a bit sardonic? A little amusement? It was something like she had a secret she couldn't wait to share. She raised her ever-present camera and took some pictures. What could she possibly see from that angle other than nose hair?

Beau suddenly felt like he was not part of a band; he wasn't part of the song. He was cast off. Adrift. She was paying attention to him. She was taking his picture.

The set called for the next song to start as the previous one ended. Beau would have preferred to take a break, hopefully long enough to get back to the ranch and pet a horse or something. Maybe stay the night and come back in the morning. It would be so much easier if she just left. However, the thought of her leaving was somehow unsettling. It felt like the entire festival would somehow become less real if she weren't there. It would feel emptier, as though there was some vital piece missing. In the middle of the chorus, Beau discovered that he wanted her to go away but stay at the same time. If she would only be willing to do that, he might be happy. That wasn't too much to ask, was it?

Camilla was staring straight at him. Her bright eyes never left his face. She didn't jump up and down like the rest but moved to the music.

Despite the fast tempo, she seemed to move sinuously. Her body rolled from side to side despite the crush of the crowd. She was breathtaking.

She was also clearly enjoying herself. As if the noises he was making, these words he sang, somehow moved her. It was a heady feeling.

The drums were nearly drowned out by the pounding in his ears. Beau's throat was parched and almost painful. Despite every effort, he could not look away from the girl. The way she danced didn't make that any easier.

He missed a few words during the next verse, not because he'd forgotten them but because his throat was so dry. They stuck there, and he had to tumble the following words out to keep the song moving. He let go of the guitar at his hip and reached for the bottle of water at his feet that he was saving for the break. The song entered an instrumental bridge where he was supposed to play a descent against the chorus. But he sat that part out as he flipped off the lid and chugged a third of the bottle.

Beau set it back down, having lost the cap, and returned to the song. Camilla's head was cocked to one side, examining him closely. She could see that he was making mistakes. Did she think less of him for it? Did she think anything of him at all?

Beau scanned the crowd. But it didn't look as though anyone else had noticed his discomfort. Most of the revelers were still dancing, mindless in their enjoyment. Most of them had also been drinking fairly heavily, a point in his favor. Somehow, perhaps through some guardian angel, Beau made it through the next song. This set called for a brief interlude, as the next song would be slow and sensual. If Camilla danced like that for the fast numbers, he feared and anticipated her movements on a slow ballad.

Beau took a deep breath to dive into the next number. But Greg, on bass guitar, was calling to check his equipment.

"Beau. Come and look at this monitor," Greg motioned him to the side of the drum kit. He was bent over a small speaker that piped sound to the band so they could hear themselves, not just the crowd or the oft-overwhelming bass drum.

"What's wrong?"

"That's what I want to know," Greg spoke to the monitor and

grabbed the top of it as though it was a questionable piece of equipment. "What's happing up there? This isn't like you. At one point, you weren't even singing the same song we were playing."

Beau winced and wiped a sheen of sweat off his face. "I honestly don't know," he sighed. He knew the other band members deserved a better explanation, and they were all gathered around the monitor now. Even the drummer had turned from his drums and leaned over to hear.

"I...there's someone in the audience I didn't expect." It was lame, but he prayed they would let him get away with that much. Let them think an old friend, a previous flame, had rattled him. Hell, half of them there had to have seen Carolyn wandering around by now. Let them think it was here.

"Who?" Tommy insisted. There was something about bass players. They couldn't let things go unexplained. It was the nature of the breed. The problem was that this particular bass player also knew Beau inside out. There was no way his mind was going to Carolyn. He knew how Beau felt about her. The fact that he was scanning the audience with an apparent interest made it clear something was up.

Beau blew out a breath. No way anyone would let this go until he gave them some kind of answer. He glanced in the direction of where he'd last seen Camilla. Maybe he'd be lucky, and she'd have gotten bored and left. Or went to get a beer like half the audience was doing. Or something. ANYTHING to avoid taking this conversation any further.

Tommy followed his gaze. "Which one is it?" he smiled.

"The girl down front with the camera. Don't all look at once," Beau panicked.

They all looked at once.

Greg whistled appreciatively. "Damn, son. She's gorgeous."

"You afraid of pretty women, boss?" Tommy grinned. "You're the lead singer! You're supposed to draw them in for the rest of us."

"You're married," Beau reminded him.

"Greg isn't, and Bob there..." he shot the drummer quizzically. "I'm not sure. Bob?"

Bob looked up with the same expression his dog wore when being scolded for chewing on his boots. "Are we done? My set sheet says we have a bunch more yet."

"Good focus," Greg grinned and slapped Beau's shoulder. "Look. Pretty girl. Good music. Whatever you're freaked about isn't going to happen while you're on stage. Make music with your friends. Enjoy the view and just play."

Beau took a deep breath and landed a soft punch on Greg's arm. "All right. Bob, take us to the ballad."

Bob grinned, picked up his brushes, and began to coax a soothing, sensual beat from the top hat of his drum set. Beau turned and found a genuine smile as he returned to the mic. It was one of the ballads he particularly liked, one he'd written himself. It started slow and moved into heartache, betrayal, sadness, redemption, and new love, and ended with a flourish of promise and laughter.

Camilla moved to the rhythm with a slow, full-body shimmy. Her eyes closed, and she was lost in the music. Greg was right. It was an incredible view.

Beau sang as he'd never sung before. She wasn't there for the band. He wasn't there for the crowd. He sang to her. She danced for him. Come what may, the rest of the set was between them and them alone.

Fourteen

IT WAS obvious that the band members had been talking about her. They weren't exactly being subtle. Every head swiveled toward her simultaneously. If there was any doubt in the tone of the conversation, the long wolf whistle had pretty much settled it for Camilla.

Ironically, she thought she had made a fool out of herself last night at the concert. This thought plagued Camilla the instant she awoke the next morning. An idea that stayed with her through her shower and morning routine. That whistle. The look on Beau's face when the guys started ribbing him about his superfan.

Argh. Can I look any more like an idiot with this guy?

Not that she should care. Of course, she shouldn't. He was a player. The women around him...Camilla needed to remember the women to snap herself back to reality. There had been so many of them. Soooo many. Two she'd seen, and who knew how many she had not. And yet she'd still stayed through the entire set until the embarrassing whistle. And even after. Why had she stayed, knowing they had been looking at her? Knowing they knew she was there for them?

Had she wanted them to know? Was she broadcasting her interest as though, by being there, she could lay some claim on Beau in front of his bandmates, who must have seen something in her the way they'd whistled? The question was, had Beau seen what they had?

And why did she need him to? He must have seen; he had sung that ballad directly to her. Camilla would have to have been blind not to notice, not to feel the connection between them as he sang and she... well...danced. She had completely forgotten to take pictures for the rest of the night.

"Stop it. Just stop it," she scolded herself.

Thoroughly irritated with herself, Camilla finished applying her makeup and checked herself in the mirror. Regardless of how she'd presented herself yesterday, she needed to be a professional today. She wanted some pictures around town. And if she were lucky, she could perhaps get into some of the surrounding areas. Life on the Great Plains was more than festivals, after all. It was the pictures of daily life that people would gravitate toward the most. People wanted to see what resonated the most deeply within themselves.

This meant that Camilla would absolutely NOT be running into Beau Rivers anytime today. His daily life involved ranches and livestock, hardly the kind of thing she expected to see today if she stuck to Cheyenne.

The only problem was the matter of her rental car. That whole incident with the tire still needed to be resolved. Camilla grabbed her rental agreement and sank on the side of her bed to dig through the fine print until she found what she was looking for.

Unfortunately, even this task turned out to be more complicated than she expected.

"We're sorry for the inconvenience. But the soonest we can swap out the cars for you would be closer to noon." The woman at the rental company's other end of the line sounded apologetic. But based on her steely tone, it was clear she would not be moved.

Not that Camilla didn't try. "Noon? What am I supposed to do in the meantime? I'm here for work...."

But even her explanations couldn't dislodge company policy. They would send out a new car when they came to pick up the old one. They would be happy to leave the keys at the front desk and were throwing in an upgrade for the inconvenience, which was something at least. It still didn't solve her transportation problems.

Already flustered and out of sorts, this was all just icing on the cake. Camilla grabbed her keys and stormed down to the hotel's reception desk to ask if they could hang onto them for the rental people and accept the keys for her new car while she was out. Thankfully, the manager was more than accommodating. He acted as though the request was ordinary, which either said something about the local car rental agencies or the man's ability to adapt to even the strangest request.

"I still need to get around town today. I wanted to get some pictures of the local murals I've heard so much about," Camilla said, lifting her camera bag instead of giving a longer explanation. "Do you have Uber here?"

The corner of the man's mouth twitched, and a chuckle escaped before he could stop himself. "I think you will find that you have several options for transportation in the meantime. The local stagecoach service might not be the most reliable. Still, I expect you'll find several car companies, public transit, or even as you say, 'Uber' or other such services happy to ferry you around town. You might also want to visit some of our galleries and museums if you are interested in art." He pulled several brochures from the nearby display the other clerk had tried to interest her when she'd checked in. Feeling guilty that she hadn't paid attention to them earlier, Camilla glanced at the brochures as the manager handed them to her. "Also, we can help you book tickets if you're interested in the performing arts. Several selections might interest you, not to mention live music. We have some excellent places where you can dance to country music--"

Live music! Already embarrassed by her faux pas with Beau, the mere mention of watching another cowboy crooning into a microphone was enough to send Camilla scrambling. "I'll think about that, thank you. If you could...um...just let me know when my car arrives. I think I'll take a walk this morning. It looks like a rather glorious day, doesn't it?"

Camilla left quickly before he could make any more suggestions. The sun felt bright, and the sky was an impossible blue. She knew this had something to do with the altitude and wished she'd taken the time to use a foundation with sunblock. Sunscreen later. It's time to soak in some culture. The galleries sounded interesting. Already she was thinking in terms of contrast: the cowboy culture against the aesthetic of fine art. It would also be interesting to showcase the modern world of the Great Plains.

A few taps on her phone engaged a car to take her where she wanted to go this morning. She spent the time waiting by looking at the brochures in her hand, surprised to see perhaps an aspect of the story she might have missed when she'd done her initial research for this trip. There was a vibrant art community well worth exploring.

Enthused about her work again, especially since this was clearly a place to take pictures where she had literally no chance of stumbling over Beau, Camilla scrambled into her Uber the moment it stopped. In no time at all, she was on her way to find some local color in the form of the giant murals which dotted the business sector of town.

Camilla got out of the car next to a giant cowboy boot decorated brightly with a vibrant painting of an antelope. A little further on, she saw other designs, each one unique and exciting. According to one of the brochures the manager had given here, there were twenty-five such boots scattered all over the city. She also wasn't the only one photographing them.

"We're here on a scavenger hunt," one young woman told Camilla while watching her toddlers trying to climb the 8-foot-tall statues. "Every week, we hunt for a different boot and post pictures on Instagram," she grinned. A few quick taps on her phone brought up the app to show her pictures to Camilla. "Nothing as fancy as you probably take with your camera. But it's fun, and the family enjoys seeing the kids."

"Do you mind if I take your picture?" Camilla asked, quite taken with the trio. The mom quickly agreed, only too happy to pose with her children for a change with the unusual backdrop. Camilla thanked her profusely afterward. The woman paused as she buckled the toddlers back into their strollers.

"Do you have kids?" she asked. "You're so good with them."

Camilla laughed. "Hardly. I take pictures of lots of children, though."

Her laugh felt false as Camilla watched them get ready to stroll away.

For the first time, Camilla considered what it would be like to have children of her own and take them on fun outings. It was a startling thought, which led to a rather detailed image of who the father of those children might be. Camilla shook her head, trying to erase the cowboy from her mind. She did not need Beau to interfere with her thoughts while trying to do her job.

Her expression must have conveyed some of what she felt, for the young mother put out a hand to pat Camilla awkwardly. "Hang in there. It'll work out with him. The best men usually start out complicated."

Complicated? Complicated didn't begin to describe it. For the past two days, Camilla had been caught up in a fantasy involving one very unavailable cowboy. Laughing, Camilla brushed off the comment and took down the young woman's contact information so she could send her the pictures she'd taken of them and went on her way.

Oddly enough, the young woman wasn't the last one to have something to say about Camilla's dating situation.

"Oh, aren't you married?" asked a pair of teenage girls, who stared at Camilla's left hand as though the noticeable lack of a ring was a crime against nature.

"No ring? Does this mean you're available?" a grizzled cowboy asked with a hopeful drawl as he leaned against one of the famous downtown murals, smoking a cigarette.

Camilla was used to this kind of flirtation. "Only for the next few minutes while I take your picture," she replied and launched into her spiel, explaining her assignment.

The day became more and more surreal from there. It seemed just about everyone Camilla talked to had only one thing on their minds: whether or not Camilla was firmly attached or at least in a significant relationship with someone. After a while, she became so sick of this line of questioning that she started making up answers on the spot.

"Does your husband have a hard time with how much you must have to travel with a job like yours?" asked a grandmotherly woman walking with an enormous dog.

Camilla fended off the slobbering advances of the dog with a grin. "He hasn't complained so far!" she quipped as she made her escape.

"A pretty thing like you unmarried? I don't understand it!" exclaimed a pair of middle-aged matrons who fussed over her as though she were one of their own daughters.

"The surgery paid off, didn't it?" Camilla replied and almost laughed when the ladies just about fell over each other in their eagerness to spot what she had 'worked on' – an impossible task, given Camilla's flawless skin and the fact she was lying through her teeth just to escape.

"So amazing..." they murmured to one another and nodded sagely to each other as they went on their way after their pictures had been taken. "I can't imagine her alone for long!"

The problem was that the jokes were wearing thin by this point because Camilla could very well imagine herself alone. She'd been on her own for a while now. Her job made it nearly impossible to maintain any kind of real relationship. The fact that she had even entertained any sort of feelings for Beau was dangerous, she knew, not just to her peace of mind but to her career. When a pair of shopkeepers across the street from the gallery she was headed for hinted that she might enjoy settling down with a Wyoming cowboy, her heart gave such a wrench that she could barely breathe.

Nonsense. I'm falling into one of my own little fantasies. Focus on something real. Something more interesting.

But the artists Camilla had hoped to find were unavailable. Sure, she could view their work at the gallery. But pictures of art weren't what made life on the plains fascinating. It was the creation and the creators of the work that mattered. The gallery owner was quite smitten with the idea of Camilla photographing local artists at work but was at a loss as to whom she might find on such short notice.

"I can leave some messages and see who gets back to you," the woman offered, trying hard to find a solution that would work for all of them. After all, any artist from her gallery who was featured was sure to bring attention to the place where this artist's work was already for sale.

"I would appreciate that, thank you," Camilla said, accepting the woman's business card with a somewhat forced smile. She understood this was entirely on her for not thinking of this angle ahead of time. She lingered near a sculpture that made her think of water for some reason, amused to find it was appropriately named "Thirst." Camilla was jotting down the sculptor's name when the door behind her opened, and a woman swept in as if she owned the place. For all Camilla knew, she did or at least might have been a partner to the woman she'd just been talking to.

"Dani, I have GOT to take you to lunch so we can talk. Last night Beau and I—"

Beau! The name alone was enough to get Camilla's attention. Of course, this woman could be talking about a hundred other Beaus. Or a thousand. Who knew how many men had the name of Beau in a city like Cheyenne? Maybe one lived on every street corner.

When Camilla turned her head to regard the newcomer, she did not doubt which Beau the woman was referring to. Camilla recognized the blonde immediately. She'd last seen her grasping the hand of Beau Rivers as though he would somehow escape the second she let go.

Or had he been the one clutching at her?

Either way, this situation was fast going from bad to worse. Camilla needed out. Now.

In the meantime, Dani, the gallery owner, tried explaining to the newcomer why she wasn't going anywhere just yet.

"Carolyn, you know I can't just leave. In fact, I was just talking to this photographer—"

Camilla wasn't going to say anything. She was already halfway to the door, slipping out entirely unnoticed. But her mouth got the best of her, the words falling from her lips before she could even think what she was doing. "Photojournalist. I'm a photojournalist. Not a photographer. Doing a piece for Geographic Insight Magazine."

Both women were staring at her. The newcomer...Carolyn, was it? She was already stepping forward, her eyes narrowing, gaze flipping between the camera around Camilla's neck and Camilla's face. There was something feral, even predatory, in her gaze.

The other woman, Dani, was still working to process what Camilla had just said. "Isn't that really the same thing?"

"Actually, no, it's not. A photographer just takes pictures. A photojournalist tells a story."

Why was she still talking? Oh yes, because it was easier to ignore the blonde circling her like a shark scenting blood in the water.

"I know you."

The words Carolyn spoke came out almost as a growl. Camilla started, even though she was half expecting the inevitable confrontation by now.

"I couldn't say we've been introduced. I only just got into town yesterday. Though you might know my work? I've been in quite a few popular magazines. My headshot always accompanies my work."

This was true and apparently impressive enough for Dani to start scrolling through her phone. "I might be able to talk one of my artists into seeing you..." she murmured, pausing on a name and punching the button to dial.

"I know I know you. It'd be impossible to forget. You had that camera of yours pointed at my boyfriend all night," Carolyn continued to stalk her prey.

"I'm a photographer...photojournalist. It's what I do. I take pictures. Especially of people whom I find interesting."

Carolyn took a step toward her, drawing herself up and shaking out her hair as if sheer volume would be intimidating. "And you're saying you found my boyfriend interesting?"

"Well, I certainly didn't find you interesting. Otherwise, I might have been taking pictures of you."

Okay, well, maybe she shouldn't have said it. But the way this woman almost tiptoed, despite the way she was already teetering on the highest heels Camilla had ever seen just to bully her ...well, it was getting to her.

Whatever the case, Camilla's words had met their mark because Carolyn had just about lost it.

"What. Did. You. Just. Say."

It wasn't a question so much as a firm statement designed to let Camilla know Carolyn knew precisely what was just said. She had probably worked out the subtext as well, which was pretty good, considering how much of an airhead Carolyn appeared to be.

Something Camilla would do well to remember if she intended to continue this battle of wits. Which she didn't.

"I said, you'll have to excuse me. I have another appointment. Dani...it was Dani, wasn't it? Thank you again for showing me around your gallery. I'll be in touch." With that, Camilla took the high road, something she should have done from the start. She might have even succeeded at it had Carolyn not spoken as she did to Camilla's back just as she reached the door.

"You and your little pictures. As if a frumpy little photographer could possibly catch the eye of someone like Beau. You're so far beneath him; I'd be embarrassed to be caught mooning over him the way you were last night if I were you. Tell me, will the picture you took of my boyfriend keep you warm at night? Is it able to touch you in ways that make you scream?"

Camilla stopped dead. It was the condescension in Carolyn's voice that finally got under her skin. "Ew. Just...ew." Camilla turned around slowly, the camera case bumping against her hip in a familiar way, which was reassuring as though she needed to gird herself for battle, and having her Nikon near to hand made her somehow stronger.

No. Not somehow. Camilla reminded herself that she'd taken pictures that had changed lives. She brought attention to disasters. Her pictures opened the eyes of people who could make a real difference in a global sense. A portrait she'd taken of a world leader had saved an election in a small country. The pictures of war orphans had been the birth of an incredible foundation that brought children into new homes. What had this silly girl ever done?

"Look," Camilla smiled. It was a dangerous smile, one with bite. "This camera enables me to see things few other people would notice. It sort of helps me to bring into focus what you might be too close to see. So, consider it me doing you a solid when I tell you...he's just not that into you. In fact...I'd say he has no interest in you whatsoever."

"What?" Carolyn blinked at her, suddenly confused.

The deer in the headlights look answered the question Camilla had been plagued with all day. She'd been right about that death grip on Beau's hand. He really had been trying to get away.

Now it was Camilla who was on the offensive. She took a step toward Carolyn the way Carolyn had stepped toward her a moment ago. "Besides," Camilla continued; her voice was soft enough that Dani probably didn't even hear. But then, Dani was still looking for contacts on her phone, so it didn't matter what Camilla said. "I know Beau better than you think. I know how much he loves steak and where he loves to order it from when he's on the road. I know he hates having attention drawn to him, and I even respect that, unlike you. All you've ever done was push him into the spotlight when he'd much rather stay out of the camera's eye."

This was a guess. But the way the blood drained from Carolyn's face told Camilla she was on the right track. Camilla took another step, feeling daring. Powerful. This feeling took her over the precipice into the lie she knew she shouldn't tell but couldn't resist. She told herself she was playing a game, like when people asked about her dating life. But Camilla knew better even as she opened her mouth to speak. "I know more than you think. But then I would. Because my sweet girl. You might think you're dating him, but you're not. I'm the one Beau keeps warm at night. Not you."

Okay, the last bit might be really over the top, but it felt good to say it. Besides, was it a lie when thoughts of him really had warmed her quite thoroughly last night when she hadn't been able to sleep?

"You're lying. I'm calling Beau."

Carolyn grabbed her phone while Camilla's momentary elation abandoned her and left something akin to panic in its wake. Time to get while the getting was good. Carolyn was already looking down, trying to get her phone's home screen to unlock, and Dani was talking on her own phone, no doubt trying to get another artist interested in Carolyn's article. Well, no time for that. It hadn't been in the original plan anyway. Camilla spun on her heels and grabbed for the gallery door. While behind her, she could hear Carolyn's phone faintly ringing in her hand.

Beau. She would talk to Beau and tell him everything she'd just said.

With her heart in her mouth, Camilla hit the sidewalk almost at a run, wondering what it was about Beau Rivers who brought out the absolute worst in her.

Fifteen

"THAT WAS some fancy singing last night." Joe bent down and tapped for the horse's leg. The mare shifted her weight and allowed him to cradle the hoof against his shin. He took the rasp and began smoothing the hoof, knocking off the sharp edges.

"Thanks, Joe." Beau grabbed a hay bale and heaved it into the wheelbarrow. He pulled it to the barn door and set it, ready to take it out to the paddock. The mare whistled her discontent, sure that he'd forgotten her there, thus forgetting to give her the bale.

"That there ballad you boys did," Joe set the hoof on the hoof jack and began to shave around the fresh trim. "I heared you sing that one many a' time. But I ain't never heared you sing it like that. Like you was inspired by 'sumptin."

Beau knew that if Joe could pick up on that, others could too. Had he been staring at her all night? He couldn't remember. Though about the only memory Beau truly had of the concert was Camilla. He had pointed her out to the rest of the band. Had they been staring at her all night too?

Greg had taken the lead on two of their songs that were slightly out of Beau's range. And Beau had taken secondary guitar. That had given him more time to watch her dance. And she had seemed to know it. She was still on his mind...

"Boss?"

Beau realized he'd been standing there with hay hooks in his fists. He had forgotten how many bales he'd stacked in the wheelbarrow while woolgathering. He slammed the hooks into another bale and hefted in on the top of the first one. He set the hooks on a peg on the wall of the barn and wheeled the hay out to the paddock.

"Boss? How many horses you feedin'?"

Two bales for four horses was enough for a couple of days. Beau tried to bring himself back to the present. "There's no rain for the next couple of days," he called over his shoulder, "Gonna let them free feed for a while."

Beau didn't know if Joe believed him or not. But it was the story he was sticking to. He cut the twine and began throwing hay over the paddock to a chorus of whinnies and snorts as the horses dove to grab the fodder.

He paused for a moment, leaning on the top rail, and reached out to stroke a horse's neck while she nibbled the grass.

It's over. It was a lovely night. Greg was right; for the moment, I got to enjoy myself and watch a pretty woman dance. But that was last night. It's over; let it go, son. The memory of Camilla was safely stored away in his mind. That night was most likely the perfect night he would ever see. But the thing about perfect memories is that they are over and done.

Beau pulled the wheelbarrow back into the barn and parked it at the base of the hay bales. He felt better, clearer, and more focused. If there was some sadness about not seeing Camilla again, that was natural. But it was not something he needed to dwell on. She was a fantasy, too far out of reach. It was time to let her go.

For an hour or so, Beau found a comforting oblivion in doing chores around the ranch. There were always chores to do, always things needing to be done.

Joe had finished trimming two more horses and pulled another reluctant mare away from the hay to start on her hooves. They worked in companionable silence for a while when Beau felt his pocket shake. He reached in and pulled out his cell.

He stared at the phone as it rang and vibrated in his palm.

"Ain't you gonna answer that?" Joe looked up from the proffered hoof.

Beau turned to his ranch hand. Joe was pulling a rock from the frog, and both he and the horse looked unimpressed with the process.

Another glance at the number calling confirmed his first intention. "No."

"How come?" The rock popped free, and Joe released the hoof. The horse resumed her stance with a snort of indignation and a quick check to see if any grass had grown under her in the last five minutes.

"It's Carolyn. I don't want to talk to her."

"Up to you, Boss," Joe drawled. The phone rang again. "But you know if you don't answer her, she's only gonna show up here. You can't hang up on a person who comes to visit."

Beau winced. Joe was good with horses. But his people skills were often rough. Still, when the man was right, he was right. Beau punched the screen to accept the call a bit harder than he needed and Joe's right eyebrow lifted to indicate that he hadn't missed that fact. Beau brought the phone to his ear and then remembered who was on the other end. He held it a few inches away to help deaden the volume. With Carolyn, that wasn't always enough. "Yes?" He knew it was rude, but he was in no mood to be charitable. He hadn't really let the image of Camilla dancing for him go yet. The problem was that he'd sung to her. But when Greg announced the final song for the night, she'd simply vanished as if she'd never been. She was like a clumsy ghost but sexy.

"Beau?"

He stared at the phone. Why was Carolyn asking if it was him? She'd called him. On a cell phone. Who else would it be? It wasn't like he was on a party line for a cell service. And yet, she was waiting for him to verify himself. "Yes?"

"Beau. Why didn't you tell me about your girlfriend?"

Her tone made it clear that this was an accusation of some kind. The fact that she had her feathers ruffled about his girlfriend was downright confusing, however. He had no idea what in the world she was talking about. "What girlfriend?"

"Don't you lie to me, Beau!" He pulled the phone away from his ear and held it against his chest, trying to keep their conversation private though it was clear she wasn't making the same effort. Was that someone trying to talk to her in the background? He pulled the phone away from his chest and stared down at it as though it were dangerous. Which button was the volume control? He hit at whatever he thought would work and wound up taking a screenshot of the screen. A few more frantic taps made the image his wallpaper. In the meantime, Carolyn continued her harangue, heedless of his replies, or rather the lack thereof.

Joe lifted his head, and Beau tapped the MUTE button. "What wrong with her?"

Beau shook his head. "That's a long list."

"No, Boss. I mean, what's she going on about?"

"You know as much as I do." Beau glanced back at his phone, but Carolyn was still going. He was at least relieved she hadn't insisted on a video call; hearing her was bad enough. Watching as his face grew red and her mouth turned into an over-painted snarl would have been too much.

Beau unmuted the phone, though he had yet to find an opening to talk. Whatever she was going on about, she had a lot to say. It occurred to him to just hang up. But Joe was right about one thing. If he cut her off now, she'd be at the ranch soon enough, scaring the horses.

"What are you...." Beau tried to interrupt Carolyn, but it was futile. He brought the phone to his mouth and whistled like he did when herding cattle or calling a dog from far away. Loud. "WHAT ARE YOU TALKING ABOUT?"

"Don't play the innocent with me, Beau. I know all about you and that...that...floozy. I guess you didn't think I would talk to your lover, did you? All this time, you've been leading me on, and you have...."

"Leading you on?" Beau repressed a shudder.

"...I met her last night at that concert. I saw the way you sang to her. To her! How could you?"

"TO WHO?" Beau was on the edge of throwing the phone in the manure pile, and if Carolyn came up the ranch, he'd throw her in too.

"That...that..." There was a pause, and he thought he heard her ask about someone's name. When she came back, she had one for him. "Camille."

"Cam..." Beau's breath caught in his throat. "Camilla?" He wasn't asking Carolyn for clarification; he was trying to process what he was hearing. How in the world had Camilla gotten mixed up in all of this?

"She told me you were...together!"

Camilla was telling people we are dating?

"So now you're not denying it after all?" Carolyn found a new head of steam. "You admit that you've been seeing a side while leading me on the entire time?"

"I didn't...."

"You just admitted you know her!" Carolyn was starting to whine on the phone. The sound was high-pitched enough that the mare Joe was working with tossed her head and snorted. Joe gave him a look, and Beau got the message. He moved further down the barn, giving Joe and the horse a little distance so Joe could get on with what he'd been doing without Carolyn scaring the livestock from twelve miles away.

In the meantime, Beau was starting to get a little mad. And not just at Carolyn. As beautiful and sensual as Camilla was, she had no cause to go around telling people that they were a couple. A part of his brain got excited at the idea. But he shoved that aside and focused on how she could make trouble for him with people more stable than Carolyn. After all, if folks started to believe that she and he were romantically linked, then anything she did reflected on him. And right now, he didn't know her well enough to be able to anticipate whatever she was going to be doing. If she was going around claiming to be dating him, she had to be some kind of crazy.

Or smitten. Was she expounding on some kind of wishful thinking? It was kind of intriguing in a weird sort of way. Even flattering.

Either way, to straighten this all up, he first had to find the woman and set the record straight. The last thing he needed was another woman after him who had no respect for his boundaries.

Those pictures. She'd been so insistent about those pictures.

He focused on his anger. If he let that go, all there was left was a certain excitement of seeing her again.

He broke into Carolyn's tirade. "I'll find out what's going on."

"I just told you what's 'going on," Carolyn snapped at him. "And you still haven't answered me!"

Beau could have denied it, could have insisted on his innocence, or explained that Camilla was lying. But the way Carolyn was catting on, she really didn't deserve any explanation. From across the barn, Joe was hanging on every word, his eyes getting larger as Carolyn questioned Beau's integrity, parentage, and even his place in the human race. He really needed to figure out why that volume control button wasn't working.

Beau covered the mic and shot a glance at his ranch hand. "Do you mind?"

"Nah," Joe winked. "I heared worse than that in the army."

Beau winced and looked down at his phone. The way Carolyn was going on, this could take a while. He handed the phone to Joe. "I have to run into town."

"Ain't you gonna need this?" Joe pointed to the phone. Awful sounds still emitted from it, like some weird soundtrack to his life.

Beau shook his head and walked to his truck. He needed open roads and loud music to wash Carolyn from his ears. He was halfway to Cheyenne before wondering where he would even begin looking for Camilla.

He figured to start at some of the best hotels in town. Where would a beautiful photojournalist spend the night? "Anywhere she wants to." The joke didn't make him feel much better.

Her dancing stuck in his head as he drove down the long drive faster than he should have. Whether it was to stop her or just being anxious to see her again, he couldn't tell. Or maybe he just didn't want to admit it. Least of all to himself.

Sixteen

CAMILLA COULDN'T REMEMBER BEING SO tired. Usually, spending the day taking pictures was an invigorating experience. She loved talking to people and interacting with them. She'd had a great lunch at a local place after leaving the gallery before going back to wandering the city and getting a feel for what made Cheyenne different from cities in other parts of the country. To her delight, she'd been thoroughly introduced to the concept of xeriscaping at a local park, where she'd talked to a group of gardening enthusiasts about growing beautiful plants in a low-water environment.

Later, she'd even been able to visit the sculptor of "Thirst," the artist of the piece she'd admired at the gallery. That she'd received a call from anyone in the art community after leaving that mess with Carolyn was unbelievable, to say the least. Dani hadn't held any grudges, though, or was too infatuated with finding a way to drive new visitors to her gallery to let go of Camilla's idea of wanting to see an artist at work.

Camilla had to venture out of Cheyenne onto the Great Plains themselves to visit Gregory Sibanda's studio. This proved to be one of the high points of her trip, watching the artist working on his next piece. She'd gotten some incredible shots and enough information to do an artist profile if the magazine was interested.

It made for a long day, though. And right now, all Camilla could think about was taking a long, hot bath.

Sadly, even that was delayed when a woman flagged her down at the hotel's front desk who had some lengthy explanation about her rental car having been replaced. She stared as the woman detailed just how they'd taken away the old car as though these were needed details when really all Camilla needed right now was the keys to the new one so she could be on her way.

"So, you're saying there was some complication I needed to know about?" Camilla finally broke in, trying to help the girl get to the point a little faster.

"No, not at all! I was just explaining how they clipped the planter when they loaded the old car on the tow truck—"

Camilla's eyes went wide as she imagined damage to the car, which she might somehow have to pay for. She had the insurance on the vehicle, didn't she? "Did they damage the car?"

"Oh, they gave me something to let you know it wasn't your fault at all and that you wouldn't be charged. Besides, it was hardly noticeable."

"So, I'm good? I don't need to worry about anything with the car?" Camilla's heart started again.

The girl stared at her. "Of course! That's what I was saying! You don't have anything to worry about at all!"

Then why worry me about it? Camilla kept the question to herself, accepted the keys to the new car, and trudged wearily to the elevator. By the time she got to her room, she only wanted to sleep.

Shower. Then sleep. A nap was going to be necessary if she was going to be able to take pictures of the city's nightlife later that evening. Further looking at the brochures made Camilla realize her aversion to live music was silly. She couldn't avoid things that reminded her of Beau forever. But if she was going to be at her best tonight, a nap really needed to figure strongly into her near future.

She fumbled the key in her hand, nearly dropping it, and entered the room. So tired, she just dropped the camera case on the floor next to the door before staggering across the room and tumbling into bed. Somehow, she managed to set it on the desk before falling face-first onto the mattress, drawing the pillows to her, already giving up entirely on any idea she had of a shower at all.

Later. I can wash the grime of the day off later.

The problem was, now that she was no longer in motion, her mind would not allow her to rest. As good as it felt to be still, her mind was racing on without full participation. Rolling over, she stared at the ceiling until she could no longer take the room's silence. She fumbled for her phone with one hand, pressing the button to call Ann almost automatically.

"Let me guess. You did it again," her best friend said by way of greeting.

Camilla groaned, throwing one arm over her eyes to block out the brightness in the room. Why in the world had she gone out and left the drapes open like that?

"Is it really that bad, or have you lost the ability to form words? Don't tell me you saw him again, forgot how to speak, and are calling me to help you remember how words work. We'll start simple. Something like, 'I want you' should make it pretty clear...."

"Ann, will you shut up a moment!" Camilla shouted, laughing.

"Ah, there you are. Want to tell me about it?"

Camilla really didn't. And did. That was the thing about best friends. You had them so you could tell them all the embarrassing stuff. Hopefully, so they could help you untangle it and find a way to make things right.

Sometimes, you had to get them to stop laughing long enough to be helpful. Camilla was only five sentences into her recitation of the whole Carolyn incident before Ann lost it.

"Ann, if you could just shut up long enough to...."

"I'm sorry, Camilla, but you really do get yourself into messes lately. Is this Beau guy really that special?

"I don't know. There's something about him."

"I'd say so, given how often you've called me about him," Ann said in such a way; Camilla could hear the smirk in her voice.

"This call isn't about him. It's about Carolyn."

Ann snickered. "Keep telling yourself that." She took a breath, and Camilla could almost hear her thinking. Ann was like that, sometimes picking through her words carefully and trying to come up with the nugget of wisdom Camilla needed most.

This time though, she came up short.

"Look, Camilla, I think you'll have to sort this out on your own. Not that I'm abandoning you or anything. But I've never seen you like this. You've always been so driven to get the story. This distraction...well, it's something new, and I'm not entirely sure what to make of it. I mean, I'm here for you, and I'm willing to listen if that helps. But maybe you need to talk more to yourself and figure out what you really want. If this cowboy has you this twisted up in knots, though, I'm thinking you've got unfinished business with him you need to resolve." Anne paused, and her voice became softer, as though she were smiling. "I'm here for you whatever you decide, you know."

"So, you think I should pursue him?"

"I think you'll only be there briefly, and Cheyenne is a large city. Really, what are the odds you're even going to see him again?"

"You just told me I have unfinished business with him. Don't I need to see him to resolve it?"

"Hey, I just dispense the advice. It's up to you what you do with it."

Camilla was amazed at how five minutes of conversation had helped her feel better. By the time she hung up, she didn't feel so awful or so foolish. After all, as Ann had finally reminded her, she wouldn't be in Cheyenne much longer. She'd made a valid point. What difference did it make what she told anyone when she wasn't likely to see either Beau or even Carolyn ever again? And even if she did have the awful luck of running into either at some club or another, it didn't mean anything. She could simply leave. If it got really bad, she could set off on the next leg of her journey a day early. There was a lot more to the Great Plains than just Wyoming. She had other places to visit and a weekend at a dude ranch just to get the full Western flavor of things coming up. Maybe she could change her reservation and come early or something.

Maybe resolving all these weird feelings had more to do with walking away with them than having any kind of confrontation. Keep the memory of the cowboy as that, a memory. Eventually, when everything wasn't so raw, this whole adventure would make a good story. Or at least an exciting segment of her project on the Great Plains.

Feeling more settled than she had all day, Camilla let the phone drop onto the bed next to her and rolled over, punching the pillow into a more comfortable shape. Right now, what she needed was a nap. Maybe she could find something more entertaining to chase than grumpy cowboys in her sleep.

But the grumpy cowboy wouldn't let her go. He chased her into her dreams. She saw him again on stage, crooning into the microphone. His eyes were on her as though she were the only woman in the world. Except he wasn't really singing. He was shouting her name. Over and over again, with so much urgency, she startled herself awake.

Camilla woke from her nap only to realize that Beau Rivers really was shouting her name. From outside the door of her hotel room.

Oh god...

Realizing there was only one reason he might have tracked her down, Camilla pulled the pillow over her head and screamed. This couldn't be happening. Things like this were supposed to be impossible. Weren't there laws against sharing information about which hotel room a person was in?

That chatty front desk person. The girl who had nothing better to do than make a story out of a rental car and a planter take ten minutes to tell. Camilla could only imagine what she'd told Beau about the guest who carried around a camera case the size of a backpack everywhere she went.

"Camilla, are you in there?"

Camilla groaned. "Go AWAY!"

There was a pause. For one long, awful moment, Camilla thought he might have actually listened to her. She sat up cautiously and listened. When Beau spoke next, his voice was softer. Less mad and more...defeated?

"Okay...but then, how will you know why I'm here?"

She did know. That was the problem. It had to do with Carolyn because, to her way of thinking, the man had no reason to be chasing her down unless he was mad, which would make Camilla crazy if she actually got out of bed and went to the door to open it.

Which she did. Or tried to do.

Instead, what really happened was that she launched herself from the bed so fast that she tripped on her discarded shoes, falling headlong into the table. She only just righted herself by grabbing the chair and stumbled into the door so hard the whole thing shook from the impact. Somehow, she righted herself. But the clip that held her hair back was lost somewhere, and she had to shove a hand through the strands to see so she could open the door.

Then Beau was standing there in front of her. Camilla's hand fell away, her hair tumbling down around her shoulders. Lips parted, and Camilla struggled to breathe properly as she stared at him, unsure he was real.

He, likewise, stared at her, his Adam's apple bobbing as he swallowed once, hard.

Many things went through her head at that moment. Starting with how much she was glad to see him. Her heart had leaped at the mere sight of him. Now she knew just how much he had come to mean to her in a matter of a day or two. There was so much potential in their attraction. She suspected they really could be something if they only had a chance.

The second thought had to do with how mad he looked. In fact, with his eyes blazing, with his body drawn up in self-righteous indignation, it was clear he had a bone to pick with her. And she had a pretty good idea what that particular bone was about.

Camilla opened her mouth to explain as Beau seemed to be having trouble speaking. But she didn't know what to say. Especially when he looked so furious and so...something else, something darkened in his eyes as Beau stared at Camilla from head to foot. His eyes lingered on her face as though he were hungry, and she was a steak done to perfection. She shivered under his gaze, liking that she could leave him at a loss for words when she had none.

When he finally spoke, his voice was hoarse. "So...what happened to you?" he finally asked, nodding at her disheveled appearance.

Camilla glanced down at her rumpled clothes. Her hand automatically went to her hair, which was an absolute mess about her face. "You happened to me."

It was a bit too honest, maybe. But he couldn't find the words any better than she did. There was a lot of emotion in that look, and she longed for her camera as she'd give anything to capture it all so she could sort it out later. The way he gazed at her so seriously, eyes smoldering, a small line forming a furrow upon his brow. The way a smile lifted the corner of his mouth just enough to let her know he was fighting his anger and losing. The way he tipped her head to regard her, trying to figure her out, and enjoying the process in doing so while being intensely frustrated at the same time.

Or maybe he was entirely frustrated by something else, given how he stepped toward her. Or perhaps she had said the wrong thing. She had meant to be flirtatious, for a chance to resolve this strange attraction between them.

The smile disappeared. He drew himself up, becoming even taller if that were possible. His jawline went rigid, his shoulders squared. She'd obviously misread the situation entirely because there was nothing sexy or smoldering about him. He was all angry cowboy when he spoke next, each word clipped with hard edges, "Is that why you're telling all of sundry you and I are a thing?"

Seventeen

THE DOOR OPENED. For a moment, Beau lost his train of thought. He'd obviously woken Camilla from a nap. Her hair was tousled, the sort of wild look you only get from pillows. She was barefoot, still in jeans and a t-shirt.

It was her hair that intrigued him the most. It fell in waves around her shoulders and frizzed out in every direction like it was seeking some static connection to the universe. Beau swallowed the image of how it came to be in that state. He tried not to imagine her laying on a pillow, with her long tresses draped bewitchingly across her bare collarbone underneath.

"What happened to you?" Beau's words came out unbidden. Camilla's appearance was so unusual that it surprised him. He hadn't expected her to be sleepy. To be sexy.

She lifted one hand to her hair and tried to smooth it. Only her hand seemed to make things worse, and soft strands wafted further in the air. "You happened to me."

It caught his breath to hear her say that. He swallowed hard through a dry throat and nearly forgot his reasoning for tracking her down. It took an effort to bring it all back, to remember his reason for being there. He forced himself to look into her eyes and willed himself to ignore the drowsy, just-woken image before him.

He pulled himself upright and squared his shoulders. He reset his weight on the back of his heels and scowled to keep himself focused. He'd taken a similar stance in the rodeo ring once while facing down the bull. The bull had only just knocked him off and had come after him rather than doing what every bull was supposed to do by allowing itself to be herded out of the arena. That stance had saved his life then; surely, it would do no less now.

So to speak.

"Is that why you're telling all and sundry you and I are a thing?"

Beau didn't like confrontations, not with people. But this woman had gotten under his skin in a bad way. He'd driven all this way and gone to a few of the finer hotels before finding the one she was staying at. He tried to keep his eyes on hers, but it wasn't easy with that halo her hair made. Still, his words might have come out a little more harshly than he had intended because she flinched. Camilla lifted her eyes to his in a way that made Beau realize there might be more to the story.

"No, well, maybe...." Camilla sighed and stepped aside, gesturing for him to enter.

For a long moment, Beau wasn't sure if he should. She would expect an apology, and he wasn't sure he was ready to forgive. She had humiliated him, made him the talk of...well, enough people for his life to be made more complicated than it needed to be. His feet were of a different mind, though. And the next thing he knew, Beau was stepping through the doorway and into the room far enough for the door to shut behind him. Like it or not, he'd committed himself to hear her out.

Camilla drifted past him, gesturing for him to sit somewhere. He looked around, not sure what was safest. The bed was right out, obviously, meaning he had to turn his gaze to the rest of the room. It was her camera he noticed first. It rested on the table almost close enough to touch. He hadn't been entirely sure that it had been detachable from her neck. He wondered briefly how many pictures of himself she had tucked on the SD card, whether he should be worried.

No. That's not why I'm here. We already resolved that argument.

Far from providing reassurance, those words further served to underscore his anger. Clearly, they didn't get along. Beau and Camilla. City and country. Oil and water. This was just one more incident high-lighting how wrong they were for each other. Except she was still sleep-tousled and as sexy as all hell as she waited for him to take a seat. Why did she have to look at him that way? Almost desperately Beau turned away to study the rest of the room, such as it was.

Beside the bed was a small round table with two chairs offering a safe place to talk. Neither chair looked particularly comfortable; plain and black, solid in design. But Camilla was already moving to sit in one of the chairs, leaving him no choice. Beau took one of the chairs and sat, reminding himself he was still not satisfied with her response.

He should have stayed standing so he could be sure to keep this short.

"I have to live in this town after you're gone. You know that, right? Cheyenne may not be a small town, but there is enough of a small town in it that rumors like this spread. And after a while, it just becomes common knowledge. You're gonna be off somewhere in the world taking pictures, and I'm going to be answering questions about you for years. Aside from that, folks around here will link me to you even if you're a million miles away."

Camilla looked down and nodded slowly. Beau could see the embar-rassment in the way she flushed and shifted uncomfortably in her seat. "I didn't think about that. I guess I didn't think at all. I was just angry, and I talked without thinking. That woman was just so..." Camilla appar-ently decided on being discrete and didn't finish that thought. "You're right. I mean this is your home and that bit...ah...Carolyn is your...um... friend..."

"Well, that's not entirely true," Beau shifted, leaning forward to rest his elbows on the table. "'Friend' is too strong of a word. Acquaintance, maybe. Pain in my butt?" He thought for a moment. "Stalker isn't too far removed either."

He made her laugh. That was nice. Too nice. She had a great laugh, and her smile lit her whole face.

Just like that, his ire vanished in a cloud of frizzy hair. He realized that he couldn't stay angry at her. For that matter, just maintaining his anger this far had taken a lot more effort than Beau had expected. This whole matter was a losing fight. I'm hungry. I don't even think I've eaten all day. Blame all this mess on low blood sugar or something. I'm done.

In fact, now that he was thinking about it, the idea of grabbing a bite was sounding mighty fine.

"Would you...like to get something to eat?"

The words burst out of him in a tumble before he could catch them back. He not only caught himself off-guard, but Camilla also did a double take. She blinked at him in slow surprise, with the beginnings of a smile tugging at the corner of her mouth. "I thought you came here because you were mad at me."

"Well, I suppose I was," Beau grinned. "I mean, telling folks a lie isn't a great way to get along. But I mean there are a whole lot worse things you could have said." Beau thought for a moment and added, "and if folks do get the opinion that you and I are a couple, well...I could do a lot worse."

"Oh, you could, could you?" Camilla shot him a sideways look, but her smile was even brighter than he remembered. It was like the sun coming out after a week of rain. "High praise indeed."

"I wouldn't want to give you a big head or nothing," Beau chuckled. "But you are on the gorgeous side of pretty. You gotta know that."

She actually blushed. He burned that image into his memory, not wanting to ever forget the first time he truly and even deliberately made her blush. That thought inferred there would be a second time, and Beau found himself hoping there would be many more.

He wanted to see her laugh until she couldn't breathe. He wanted to be there to dry her eyes when she cried. He wanted to see her in every mood, waking or sleeping. Okay, maybe the last thought was a little creepy. But right now, Beau couldn't get enough of her, and he wasn't altogether sure what to do with that.

"Sure." Her acceptance brought him back to the moment. She pointed to the window of the hotel room and the noise coming from the street. "Sounds like a party."

"Kinda," Beau agreed. "It's part of the festival. Like the concert. Tonight is the last night. It'll be fun."

Camilla rose and headed to the suitcase next to the bed. "I'm going to go and freshen up." She took a long look at him and added, "I take it the festival is an informal affair?"

"Come as you are," Beau agreed. She reached into her suitcase and pulled something free. He thought it was a shirt, though it was so fast, he couldn't be certain. She walked into the bathroom and closed the door, leaving him to stare after her and wait for the inevitable.

"One..." Beau whispered to himself, "two..."

Camilla's shriek came out as the word 'two' left Beau's lips. "Why didn't you tell me about my HAIR?"

Feeling like discretion was called for, Beau savagely choked down the laugh that threatened to burst out of him. But he bit his tongue to do it. In the end, the only safe thing he could think of was to find the window air conditioning and pretend to be fascinated by the simple controls in case she poked her head out of the bathroom and saw the smile he could not suppress.

'Freshening up' took longer than he expected. But compared to waiting for someone like Carolyn, it was nearly instantaneous. When Camilla returned, she was wearing a nice cream-color blouse, and her hair was pulled back into a ponytail rather savagely.

"That looks like it would hurt." Beau pointed to the flat tresses captured by a tight band.

"No." Camilla sat on the edge of the bed and slipped on a pair of shoes. "Well, a little. But I had to try and tame it down." She grabbed the camera again and seemed to consider it. In the end, she set the case back down on the table and left it there. "No work tonight." She said the words decisively and he realized she'd kind of surprised herself when she said them.

"You sure?" he asked, not wanting her to make any sacrifice on his account.

"Absolutely," she said and went to the door. She pulled it open deliberately and put her back to the camera as if it truly didn't matter. "So...where to?"

Beau shrugged, not wanting her to see how much this simple action touched him. She was letting him know she wanted to be with him tonight. Not as an excuse to take pictures of the festival but because... well whatever reason she'd agreed to go with him. Whatever it was, it felt good. He certainly wasn't about to question it. "There's a nice Greek place down the street." He gathered his hat from his hands and firmly planted it upon his head. "Also Korean, but that's a bit of a drive from here." He lifted an eyebrow at her reaction. "Let me guess, you figured it was all old west saloons and gunfights."

"No," she said the word with little conviction. It was painfully obvious that the wild west was indeed what she had been expecting.

"We save that for Sunday after services," Beau winked and took her hand as he stepped out into the hallway, tucking it through the crook in his arm. Laughing, Camilla checked to make sure the door locked behind her and followed him amiably enough down to the street and out into the world of Cheyenne at its best and rowdiest.

Camilla was a delightful dinner companion, as Beau expected she would be. They ended up at a steakhouse near the hotel and watched through the window of the restaurant as people walked through the downtown area.

"What exactly is the festival all about anyway?" Camilla sipped her wine while waiting for their steaks. "I mean I read up on it. But I'm not seeing the history part right now so much as an excuse for a good time."

Beau shrugged. "Frontier Days is a sort of homage to the Old West and the folks that settled here and made Wyoming a state. Our history is part of who we are. So while you see the locals out there having a good time, the past is always with them too. It's what made us strong enough to pursue our dreams on our own terms. Whatever they might be." Beau pointed out a horse-drawn carriage making its way down the street. The warm summer night was perfect for it and the couple snuggled in the carriage seemed delighted.

"So, there is a little of the Old West-saloon-gunfighter vibe after all."

Beau leaned past her to point out a pair dressed up as outlaws posing with the tourists. "Well, you can take the state out of the Old West. But you can't take the Old West out of the state."

When the food arrived, Beau changed the conversation to her. He wanted to know as much about her as he could while he had the chance. Her experiences as a photographer, her childhood, the exotic locations she'd been to, he asked her everything. Every story she told led to another, a series of tales that made up the framework of who she was and what mattered most to her.

He loved everything about her.

At one point, Camilla confessed that traveling had its downsides. Loneliness was the chief complaint. She stopped midway through her story and cocked her head to one side. "Why are you asking me all of this?"

Beau took a slow bite of steak and chewed it thoughtfully, letting her wait for the answer. "Don't really know. I suppose that it's the normal kind of thing that someone should know about the person they're dating, don't you?"

"Is that what this is? A date?"

"Why not?" Beau lifted his glass. "Let's put a little truth to the rumor."

She grinned and touched her glass to his. The resulting chime was pure and delicate. She sipped the wine and refused to look up at him for a long moment. "Tell me about your life here. About Wyoming, about where you live, you said you have horses..."

"Not a lot to tell. Nothing exciting anyway."

"Come on." Camilla suddenly had a wicked gleam in her eye. "Isn't this the sort of thing that a person should know about the person they're dating?"

Beau laughed. "Alright, what would you like to know?"

It sounded dull compared to her history, he feared. After all, he lived a fairly straightforward life. But Camilla seemed as enthralled with him as he had been with her. She asked lots of questions and the time passed so comfortably that it felt as though they'd known each other forever by the time dessert was served. They lingered over the wine for a while as the night settled in.

Twice someone Beau knew came into the restaurant and said 'hello' as they strolled past to get to their tables. Each one gave them both appraising looks. From their expressions, they all seemed to approve of Beau and Camilla as a couple.

Beau couldn't help but grin as they shared greetings and small talk. It was like he'd told Camilla at the hotel; he could do a lot worse.

"What's got you grinning like that?" Camilla cocked an eyebrow at him.

"Just...kind of proud to be seen with you," Beau said it straight, without trying to be shy or cute. What was the point? It was the simple truth, after all.

Beau walked Camilla back to her hotel. His truck was still in the parking lot. They took their time, wandering through the brightly lit streets and the decorated sidewalks. The city had gone all out for Frontier Days, as it always did. He walked along the outside where the curb met the street because it was the way he was raised.

They passed a business that was closed. The hour was getting late, and there was a shadow across the sidewalk. In the darkness, Camilla didn't see the uneven pavement and stumbled, her hand shooting out for balance. Beau caught her hand in his and made sure she was all right before continuing.

She didn't ask for her hand back, and he didn't want to let go of it.

She was strong. He could tell that much even though she lay her hand in his softly. There was underlying muscle there. Still, her hand was warm, her skin was soft, and her hand fit so well in his. He was a little self-conscious at first; after all, life on a ranch tends to build callouses and rough skin. But she seemed to have no such qualms.

He walked her inside. The woman at the counter was unusually quiet as she took in the pair heading to the elevator. But her smile gave away her opinion of what she saw. It seemed that everyone was fully in favor of their relationship. Though it had only really started a couple of hours ago.

Beau walked Camilla to the door and there, reluctantly, let go of her hand. "I seem to have left my phone at home," Beau said, wondering if Carolyn was still giving Joe an earful. "But..." He reached into his pocket for a pen and found nothing. He patted his pockets and realized he had nothing to write on either.

"Here." Camilla handed him her phone. She had created a new contact with the heading BOYFRIEND. He chuckled and added his phone number in the appropriate slot. After a moment, he added his address too.

"I know you said you were checking out in the morning. But if you got more time before you have to run across the world again...maybe we can find someplace else to go?" Beau took a breath and hoped he was doing the right thing when he asked, "Coffee tomorrow before you hit the road?"

Camilla grinned and answered without hesitation. "I'd like that."

He wanted to kiss her. More than anything. He wanted to be in her arms, to feel her against him. But the timing wasn't quite right. She waited. He wondered if maybe she felt it too; maybe she didn't care about the timing and just wanted to be with him.

Beau took her hand and brought it to his lips. "Goodnight, girlfriend."

Her eyebrows shot up. It was not what she had expected. But Beau was raised a gentleman, and that was what he was. He tipped his hat and headed to the elevator and didn't look back.

Besides, it had been a perfect night. He wanted to savor every moment with her.

Eighteen

IT SHOULDN'T HAVE BEEN difficult at all. He'd actually put in not only his number but his address into her phone when she'd offered it to him with that daring header. Boyfriend. Now, looking back Camilla was stunned by her audacity and wondered why he hadn't headed for the hills. On horseback no less.

But he hadn't. He'd put in his number. And now they were supposed to meet for coffee tomorrow. Before she 'left town.' Only Camilla didn't want to leave. Nor did she really have to. Her schedule was her own. She could, in theory, linger just a little longer.

A day. Only one more day, she told herself and fell backward on her bed to stare up at the ceiling because she was acting crazy, and she knew it.

He'd been mad at her. Camilla had to remember that. And she'd already acted so awfully with his ex-girlfriend. Even after an evening spent together, a wonderful evening spent together, she had to admit this whole setup wasn't normal. This wasn't how relationships were supposed to work. They were running on fast-forward, and it still wasn't enough. She'd had to make the step to calling this something more than it should be after only a couple of days.

And he'd accepted.

Boyfriend.

Camilla jumped up and paced around the room, thinking franti-cally. She eyed her phone but what could her friends tell her that hadn't already been said? Ann would give her an earful.

Maybe she needed an earful. A whole lecture designed to set her straight. Get her head back in the game before she messed up this entire assignment by getting hung up in one tiny town in Wyoming when what she really and truly needed, more than anything, was to get back on the road and discover just how big of an area the Great Plains encompassed.

Yes. That was it. She needed Ann to tell her to drop this whole thing before it got away from her.

In moments she had dialed and waited impatiently through three rings. Camilla started to think she was going to have to leave a message, or more likely, a text when Ann picked up the phone, breathless.

"Don't tell me. The cowboy hottie."

Camilla laughed at the greeting, thankful her best friend couldn't see her blushing. "How did you know?"

"I've talked to you more in the last 48 hours than I usually do in a week. Not that I mind. But you have to admit, there's a certain pattern to your most recent calls."

"Fair enough. Though right now I need a distraction. Tell me about you."

Thankfully, that was all Ann needed to take the conversation and run with it. Guiltily, Camilla realized she'd been using her friend for advice. But she hadn't exactly been showing a lot of interest in things outside her own personal crisis of late. She listened to a long story about a problem Ann was having with a mutual friend, making all the appro-priate noises, glad to bask in someone else's troubles for a while. It was easier, really. And a relief to let go of the handsome cowboy until she could (hopefully) gain some perspective.

Perspective. Ha. What she needed was to relax completely and forget him entirely for the night. Camilla knelt at the mini-fridge in her room. If ever there was a time for super overpriced alcohol, this was it. Sadly, this hotel wasn't the sort to have a minibar stacked in the fridge. It was annoyingly empty.

Why in the world did people put mini-fridges in rooms after all? Camilla slammed the door and flopped back on the bed. She must have made some noise not in keeping with the narrative because Ann stopped whatever she was saying and switched directions entirely.

"Camilla, I don't think you're even listening."

"Am I that obvious?"

"To me...yes," Ann hesitated. "Look, why don't you just talk to me about what you wanted to when you called me. I'm sure my whole little bit of drama doesn't interest you in the least. You know Patrice and I are going to make up. We always do. Even if she's a self-centered b—"

Camilla laughed. "Isn't that part of why you love her? Because she's so amazingly self-confident even if she's a little blind to those around her sometimes."

Ann grumbled but was soon giggling. "Yes. Exactly. Okay, so what's going on with the cowboy you're trying very hard to not talk about?"

"We spent the night together."

At Ann's gasp, Camilla backpedaled quickly. "Okay, wrong wording altogether. We went out. Dinner. Conversation. We had a really nice time. A REALLY nice time."

"AND?" Anne practically shrieked the word.

"And nothing. He gave me his number and told me to stay in touch. We're meeting for coffee tomorrow after I check out of the hotel."

"But you had a good time?"

"We had dinner. We talked. Later we took a walk. It was..." Camilla hesitated. Normally, she wasn't at such a loss for words. She prided herself on being able to paint a picture with the right turn of phrase, using dialogue to draw the viewer to the portion of the picture that was important. Significant.

If she put this night through the lens of the camera, what would she see? What would she want someone else to be able to see?

"He took me to a steakhouse. Again. I think all he eats is steak. But the décor...it fits him. I think he eats at steakhouses because they make him feel at home. Surrounded by rodeo memorabilia and branding irons, it's just...a part of his world that I think he wants me to see as if he wants to remind me of how different we are. It's as though he's waiting for me to come to my senses and hit the road, to run away from him as fast as I can."

"And do you want to? Run, I mean?" Ann asked, her voice soft.

Camilla closed her eyes and thought. "No. Not in the least. The more I learn, the more I want to know. He says his life isn't interesting. But I can't get enough. Not just because it's different but because it's where he is, if that makes sense. We traded stories, and I started to see him for who he is. And it made me want to find out everything about him. Every answer to a question only raised another as though I need to memorize him before I leave tomorrow."

"Do you have to?"

"Memorize him?" Camilla shut her eyes to picture him. "No. I already know him as clearly as if I could see him in one of my photographs. Which I could actually use to look at to refresh my memory if I need to, which means I'm being stupid and sentimental."

"Silly," Ann chided her. "Not, do you have to memorize him? That's already obvious. But do you have to leave tomorrow? Couldn't you give him one more day? A little bit longer, just to see..."

"...if it's real?" Camilla finished for her, her breath catching at the thought of it. "But I'm only going to get more attached. Besides, that would be silly. He only asked me to join him for coffee. He expects me to leave. If he thought I was staying, he would never—"

"You don't know that! Give him a chance. Unless...you don't think he's worth it."

"He's worth it!" Camilla snapped, then stopped when she realized what she'd just said. "Oh."

"Yes. Oh." Ann chuckled. Camilla could picture her shaking her head.

"I need to ask him out."

"You need to ask him out."

"I've never asked out a man before. They've always done the asking," Camilla protested, panicking now that she was thinking about it.

"Good heavens. What century are you living in?" Ann's voice rose almost an octave. "Do you mean to say you've never in your life ever been the one to instigate a date?"

"I um...really haven't dated all that much if you recall. I've always been too busy."

"Too busy. Camilla, you're going to busy yourself out of something magical if you're not careful."

It was true. Camilla had been putting off relationships for too long, putting her efforts into her career for so long now that she'd almost forgotten she was still a woman, not just a photojournalist.

"I'll stay another day," she said finally.

"And you'll ask him out?" Ann prodded when Camilla didn't finish the thought.

"I'll ask him out."

Nineteen

CAMILLA HAD TOLD Ann the truth last night. She had really never asked a man out before. Now, she had not only spent the night agonizing over what she was going to say when she saw Beau again, but she'd also sort of cleared her schedule for a couple of days just to spend them with him.

She was going to look mighty stupid if she didn't ask him out and wound up holed up in her hotel room, afraid to leave, lest he figures out she was still in town when she'd said she was leaving.

Yeah. Not the way she wanted this to go down.

Camilla rehearsed the words in her mind as she waited for Beau to show up for coffee. So far, she'd been through a dozen variations and hadn't liked any of them.

"Hon, can I at least get you a coffee?" The barista hovered at her elbow, sympathetic. She'd abandoned her post behind the counter just to come over and talk to Camilla, probably because she'd been sitting there at least half an hour now, waiting for Beau to show up.

No, she wasn't exactly waiting for him to show up. She'd been early, just so she wouldn't miss one minute with him. And also, she could work up the nerve to ask him out.

"How would you ask out a guy?" she asked the barista in a burst of impulsivity. "I mean, especially if you hadn't known him all that long?"

"I think I'd just come out and ask. Nothing ventured, nothing gained..." the girl answered with a sympathetic smile. "Some tea maybe instead? Chamomile, to maybe help settle your nerves?"

Camilla shot her a look. "Do I look that bad?"

"Let me put it this way. I've never seen a woman pace while sitting still before."

Okay, maybe she'd been a little jittery. "Water. Water would be fine," she murmured, as the door opened across the shop and one very tall and handsome cowboy strode in as though he owned the place. That was the most remarkable thing about Beau. He looked like he fit in wherever he went.

No. He didn't just look like it. He did.

The girl mouthed, "Is that him?" in such an exaggerated, blatant way it was a wonder Beau never noticed. But Beau's eyes never left Camilla as he came across the room to her table like he couldn't wait to get to her.

It mirrored the way she couldn't wait for him to show up. It was only through serious force that she kept herself sitting still until he got there. When he arrived, she got up to give him a hug, which somehow ended with an awkward kiss on the cheek before they both retreated to their separate sides of the table, blushing like a couple of teenagers on their first date.

It's just coffee, she reminded herself.

Except it wasn't. This simple date had the potential to become something more, if only she could open her mouth and say the simplest of words: Spend the day with me.

Instead, it was all she could do to make small talk.

"Been here long?" he asked as they settled into their respective seats.

"Only a few minutes." Of course, that was an outright lie, but he didn't need to know that. Better to distract with a compliment. "You look great!"

He chuckled at her enthusiasm. "You're pretty amazing yourself."

Camilla glanced down at her floral print blouse and brushed a nervous hand across the short denim skirt, which suddenly felt too short. She'd wanted to show off her legs, but his compliment made her self-conscious. "Thank you."

She wasn't sure what to say from there. How did you get from small talk to asking someone out on a date anyway? "Coffee. Weren't we going to have some coffee?" she asked, jumping to her feet so suddenly that her hip hit the table painfully hard and rattled the small vase of daisies that sat on the checkered cloth. She reached out to steady it the same instant he did. His fingers closed over hers, warm and strong.

Camilla couldn't breathe.

"You okay?" Beau stood so close she could feel the warmth of his breath on her cheek.

"Fine!"

He let go of her hand, fingers falling away slowly in almost a caress that seared her skin. Camilla shivered at his touch and hid it by turning toward the menu board over the long counter along one wall of the café. "They have quite an impressive menu for such a small space."

"Still expecting the Wild West?" he asked as he followed her up to order. Thankfully, she had a moment to decide as a trio of middle-aged women all carrying copies of the same book had beaten them to the register and were arguing over their orders.

"I think I know better by now. I just didn't expect quite so many specialty drinks. I count at least fifteen and have no idea what some of these are. What in the world is a 'Mountain Mocha'?" Camilla flashed a grin in his direction. "Kind of reminds me of that bewildering menu the first time we met."

"You've deduced my master plan. I'm trying to keep you wondering, so you never stop needing me."

She blinked. "Needing you..." She imagined what that would be like, the desire she already felt when he was near deepening to something more integral to who she was. As though the very act of having him near somehow made her life...better. The way it was meant to be lived.

Beau flushed and gestured at the menu board, cheeks flushed. "I mean to translate. You don't stop needing me to translate."

"Right. To translate."

Still, the image stayed with her. Is that what they could have? No...

probably not. Not if this date ended here at a friendly cup of coffee before she was supposed to hit the road.

Camilla took a deep breath, closed her eyes, and before she could talk herself out of it, said, "Do you want to go sightseeing with me tomorrow? I'll drive."

The words came out so fast it was a wonder he even understood them. But he must have because he answered just as quickly, "You'll be driving with your eyes open, I hope."

She opened her eyes only because she wasn't sure if he was laughing with her or at her. "Very funny."

The barista finished up with the book club ladies and turned toward them with a smile. "What can I get you? Water?" She directed the question at Camilla, all apologetic. "I'm sorry I didn't get back to you with that. I was suddenly swamped."

"It's fine," Camilla answered quickly with a pointed look at the barista, trying to convey telepathically that she had only just arrived in the coffee shop. And she had certainly never had any kind of conversation with her about asking a guy out.

The barista gave her a look, pursing her lips and made a lock-in-key movement with her hand, which, of course, only made everything worse. Thankfully, Beau didn't seem to notice, as he was busy staring up at the menu with as much bewilderment as Camilla had expressed when she'd first looked up at it.

"So...coffee..." Camilla leaned in to peruse the board with him. "What are you thinking?" she asked, her tone conspiratorial.

"Right now? Black coffee. Plain. I'm just not sure they can manage it. Is that mango on the menu?"

"I think that's supposed to be a smoothie," Camilla murmured, though she wasn't entirely sure.

"Black. Plain," Beau said.

The barista frowned. "No cream? Sugar? Shot of espresso? Maybe a dusting of—"

"Black. Plain," Beau repeated, crossing his arms and staring her down. Camilla swallowed a laugh.

"Right. And you?"

The poor girl looked so miserable by the simple order that Camilla took pity on her. "I'll take a Frontier Froth, extra caramel."

"Froth?" Beau stage-whispered as soon as the barista stepped back to start assembling their order.

"I think it's a latte. Or something like it. Maybe." Camilla watched in growing horror as the barista added three shots of something dark to the drink and then turned to put in a squirt of chocolate as well as caramel. "Maybe I should have asked you what that was?"

"Honey, I'm not sure anyone knows what that is."

"My pancreas might have some opinions once I drink it..." Camilla whispered and laughed at the look he gave her. "So...sightseeing?"

The barista returned with her drink. Or it might have been a drink at some time. It looked like cookie crumbles had been added to the uppermost layer, giving the drink the appearance of having been transformed to something more solid. Like a dessert.

The barista handed over the drink in barely concealed delight, murmuring, "If he says yes, an angel gets their wings."

Camilla started to laugh and took a long drink of her coffee to cover her amusement. She wound up with a face full of whipped cream and a dab of caramel syrup on her nose.

Beau raised an eyebrow and passed her a napkin as he waited for his black coffee. Plain. "I feel like I'm missing part of the conversation here."

Camilla wiped her face. "So far, you're not missing a thing," she muttered. Embarrassed, she took her cup and headed back to the table before the barista did something helpful like offer the information that Camilla had asked for her advice. Or that she'd showed up over a half an hour early for their date. "Sightseeing?"

Beau took the seat opposite her before answering. His delay didn't bode well. "Camilla..."

That did it. Camilla suddenly felt sick in a way that had nothing to do with the over-sweetened confection that was her coffee. She'd made a fool of herself and taken extra days off work for...nothing. He wasn't interested. And now here she was, stuck in Cheyenne for two more days without him. It couldn't get any worse...could it?

Oh gosh, it could. Beau took her hand. Pity. He was offering her pity.

She started to pull away. "Forget it. It was a stupid idea..." she babbled, nearly knocking over his coffee in her haste to get away.

"Camilla! Will you sit down and listen a moment?"

Camilla bit her lip and sat back in her chair again, staring resolutely at the dripping, melting mess that was her drink.

"I was trying to think of a way to tell you that I'd set up some meetings for today. I thought you were leaving. And I wanted to...well, keep busy. So, I wouldn't miss you so much when you were gone. I would be delighted to spend the day with you sightseeing. But now I'm not sure how to get out of things. There's a breeder of bulls I've been trying to get in to see for ages..."

Camilla looked up in startled wonderment. "Really...? You wanted a distraction?"

Maybe it was a strange thing to feel flattered by. But it was definitely a step in the right direction.

"I don't need to leave just yet," she told him, reaching across the table to take his hand. "I mean, if you're available tomorrow maybe? I reworked my schedule. I...um...wasn't quite ready to leave you and sort of rearranged things to give me a couple extra days..."

"You have tomorrow?" His eyes lit up with excitement.

She nodded.

"If you don't mind waiting..."

"Not in the least. I could use a day to sort through the pictures I've already taken. I have a handful of SD cards to go through."

Beau smiled. "Then it's a date. Tomorrow, I mean. On the condition that you let me drive."

"You drive? What's wrong with me driving?"

"Lady, I've seen you drive," he said, lips twitching with suppressed laughter.

It was impossible to be mad. Not when he looked the way he did, happy and boyish in his delight. "Deal," Camilla said and toasted him with her Frontier Froth, sloshing a good-sized dollop of whipped cream right into his open cup of plain black coffee.

Twenty

THE TRUCK CLICKED as the engine cooled. Beau sat for a minute and stared at the hotel entrance. It don't get easier by putting it off. Beau took a deep breath and grabbed the rear-view mirror to check himself once more. The collar lay perfectly on the right, but the left side kept sliding down, it made him look like a confused dog.

He pulled it straight and propped it against his shirt, but it only slid down that much slower. It probably needed ironing or starch or some kind of...staple. Unfortunately, life on a ranch wasn't naturally inclined to garment care. Beau gave up and faced his reflection. "She knew you for a cowboy when she met you," he reminded himself. "'Least you're not covered in hay." He gave himself a quick check to make sure he wasn't covered in hay and hopped free of the truck cab.

Getting into the hotel and to Camilla's floor was easy. But a touch of nervousness caught him at her door. He schooled himself sharply and knocked. Beau shoved away the touch of uncertainty as he waited for her answer. It was stupid to be nervous. After all, she was the one who'd asked him originally. That she wanted to go out with him was a sure thing.

The door opened, and it was like spring walked out of the room.

Camilla wore a light summer dress that came just above her knees and thin straps over her bare shoulders. She sported cowboy boots, the kind that were never meant to see the rough side of a ranch. Her hair was loose around her shoulders. All current thoughts vanished from his mind at the sight of her. And the view got even better. Her smile at seeing him was like the sun coming out in a clear blue sky. It touched her eyes and when she said, "hello."

Beau realized that he was staring at perfection. Not her, or rather, not just her, but the moment, the greeting, the perfection of that instant. No matter what happened, it would be indelibly burned in his memory for the rest of his life.

It took a second look before he noticed the camera slung around her neck and under her arm. He felt a bit like sighing, but it turned into a chuckle. She was a photographer, and a good one. Getting her to leave that behind would be as impractical as making him work the ranch without his gloves or the knife he kept for cutting hay bales and pulling rocks from hooves. It was part of her; and thinking about it that way, it was endearing.

If she had to remember that he was a rancher, then he had to remember she was a photographer. Beau reached up and smoothed down the half of the collar that had been behaving.

"Are you laughing at me?" Camilla sounded coy, almost playful.

"No ma'am. You...you're beautiful. You just took my breath away for a moment."

She smiled brighter but cocked her head slightly to the left. He was beginning to understand that was what she did when she was analyzing him. "You're sweet." Camilla reached around and held the camera in between them. "But I think you're laughing at my camera." She shrugged, and he noted the lines of her shoulder as it rose and fell.

"Well...I supposed I was a bit," Beau confessed. She was quick and very smart. There was no use denying his initial reaction. She'd seen him and noted his initial pause.

"What can I say? I'm a photographer."

"Yes. You are. And a damn good one from what I hear. 'Course, you'd have to be to make a living at it."

"You don't mind?" She tilted the camera a bit, to show him she was actually asking if it was alright to bring it. He was touched that she would even consider going without it for his sake.

"Nah. I don't mind a bit," Beau thought a moment and added quickly, "on one condition." He let a slow smile build across his lips. "I want at least one picture of you from today."

"Of me?" Camilla set the camera back where it slung at her hip, "or of us?"

"Both."

She laughed and called him "greedy" and locked her door. "So where are we headed today?"

Beau gave her a look. "Isn't that for me to know and you to find out?" he asked, unable to resist teasing her just the littlest bit.

"It helps to know if I'm dressed right for the day."

"If you don't mind walking a little," he said, with a wary glance at her shoes. "Not far."

She gave him a look. "Now I'm intrigued." They paused in the hallway as someone tried to get past them with an overburdened luggage cart. They both wound up pressed against the wall and were laughing again by the time they straightened. He looked in concern at the camera case that had been wedged between them.

"Let me carry that for you."

Camilla gave him a long appraising look. "Aren't you the gentleman?" She slipped it off her shoulder and handed it carefully to him. It occurred to him that she was entrusting him with what was likely the most valuable thing she owned. Not just the price of the camera, but the fact that she relied on it for her living. Beau very carefully hung the strap over his shoulder and held out his elbow. She took the proffered elbow, and her hand on his arm filled him with a certain pride. Beau found he couldn't stop smiling.

They had to turn around in the elevator, and she was forced to let go of his arm. When the doors opened, he placed his hand on the small of her back, waiting to be sure she didn't object. She nestled into his touch, and he walked beside her, his hand comfortably on her back.

They didn't go out to the truck immediately, though. He detoured to the hotel restaurant on the first floor where they already had several bags waiting for him.

"Now I'm really intrigued," Camilla said as she juggled two of the bags while he handled the rest along with her camera with ease.

"Do you like picnics?"

Her eyes widened in what he hoped was delight. "I love them. Where are we headed?"

"I thought we would start the day at Curt Gowdy State Park. Maybe find a place not far from the road to enjoy some lunch. You could grab some nice pictures out there if you have a mind to."

"Is that the one with the four waterfalls?" she asked, and he smiled when he realized she'd done her research.

"Yes ma'am. But that's a bit more of a hike..."

"Hang on...I'm changing into something better for hiking..."

And just like that, he wound up with all three food bags thrust into his arms while his date disappeared back inside the hotel at a dead run.

Beau shook his head and busied himself with packing the lunch and camera in the truck. To his surprise, Camilla was back in minutes, having switched out her cowboy boots for hiking boots which had obviously been well loved, the leather creased but still sturdy and comfortable. These boots had seen some use, and he realized just how hard she worked to get the pictures she did.

"I'm ready!" Camilla sang out and flung a tote bag in the back of the truck. "I brought the other boots in case we decide to do something else later," she said, and he loved the enthusiasm in her voice. This was a woman who loved adventure and wasn't afraid to try new things. It was going to be a wonderful day.

And just like that, Beau felt something lighten within him. The day was definitely looking like...well, like it was a day to really get to know each other, in all new ways. They had a hike to look forward to, and a picnic. But more than that. It would be an opportunity for him to see how he fit in her world when she was working. It would also be a chance to see how well she fit in his because he intended to take her out to his ranch later, if she was game, and give her a glimpse into what he actually did for a living.

The parking lot of the hotel held a slight breeze, enough to ruffle the hem of her dress but not enough for her to worry about it taking more than the hem with it. Beau set a little gentle pressure on her back to guide her to the truck. Camilla responded to his touch like they had been together for years. She seemed to naturally be in sync with him.

He opened the passenger side of the truck and gave her a hand getting in. The bottom of the dress rode up just high enough to give him a glimpse of her leg, but no more. He made sure she was in, and the dress wouldn't be caught in the door as he closed it.

Climbing in behind the wheel, he settled his seatbelt and reached for the ignition, but her hand stayed his. He glanced over, confused at first, but her fingers laced through his.

He wasn't sure what to do then, afraid that anything he did might break the spell of the moment. Her long, strong fingers felt warm and wonderful in his, and he gently curled his fingers over hers.

She hadn't yet fastened her seatbelt, allowing her to slide over the bench seat just close enough to place a kiss on his cheek. He turned in surprise and got another one on his lips.

She giggled at his expression. He figured he must have looked fairly shocked, he certainly felt poleaxed. "I just thought it might be easier if we got the first kiss out of the way early," Camilla squeezed his hand tightly. "You're welcome."

"I don't know..." Beau drawled out the words, putting on his best cowboy-aww-shucks act. He could tell she wasn't buying it for a moment, but she was enjoying the show. "I think the first kiss is kind of mutual."

He set his free hand on her cheek and drew her to him. She smelled of lilac and sunshine, though how he could ever explain what that meant was beyond him. He brought her close and lay his lips on hers. Her arm snaked around the back of his head as his hand reached for her ear. He squeezed her other hand, relishing the sensation of her fingers in his.

Beau and Camilla lingered in the embrace for a long moment. They were far away from everyone, in the sanctuary of the truck. They were lost in the kiss, in each other, in the sweet rightness of the kiss between them.

When they parted, they lingered close, watching each other, looking to the depth of each other's eyes. He never wanted to stop.

She didn't let go.

He was right. It was going to be a wonderful day.

Twenty-One

IT WAS OVER.

Camilla's hands didn't want to finish the task of folding her clothes and replacing them in her suitcase. They fumbled over the task. She was dropping things. Wadded-up socks slipped out of her grasp and rolled under the bed. Her sunglasses landed on the bedside table, thankfully undamaged. The keys to her rental had disappeared altogether. One minute they were in her hand, the next they were gone. In the bed somewhere. Or maybe in the trash.

In a moment she would start crying and be unable to stop.

The problem was that Camilla didn't want to leave. Her entire body seemed in on some sort of weird conspiracy to keep her from getting to the airport on time. Now, as she tore apart her room looking for the missing keys (turning up an SD card, twenty dollars, and her favorite hand lotion in the process), she wondered what would happen if she just...stayed.

"I can't!" Camilla screamed the words in frustration, needing to hear them out loud. It didn't matter how wonderful, how magical her outing with Beau had been yesterday. She could not stay. She needed to fly to Rapid City, South Dakota to be in time for some local event or another. And then she had a meeting in Kansas City a few days later. The rest of her trip was going to be rushed because of how much time she'd already spent in Wyoming.

Not that she regretted a single minute of it. The longer she stayed, the more she realized how much there was to Wyoming. Previously, this had been one of those states she'd only flown over on her way to somewhere else. It's amazing how much one missed traveling in such a way. The state park had been spectacular, especially the series of waterfalls where they'd picnicked. Even more interesting had been the people who were taking time out to camp in the state park. Camilla had quite an interesting time talking to people from all over the Great Plains and beyond and was catching a glimmer of her next piece, focusing on those who spent their time living on the road, traveling from one place to another.

All in all, it had been a satisfying day, professionally.

Personally...

Well, it was no wonder she'd wanted to stay put to the point where she was sabotaging her trip to the next point of interest. As she redoubled her efforts to find her keys, Camilla reflected on the more important aspect of the day: her time with Beau.

Beau had been wonderful. Their kisses had been absolutely inspiring, sending a sizzle down her spine, which made her yearn to stay. But more than that, Beau was good company. He was thoughtful, kind, interesting, intelligent...he was everything that made up a good companion, with an attraction that left her seeing possibilities she never had before this moment. But Beau was a man tied to the land he worked. You couldn't just up and move an entire ranch on a whim. That meant if Camilla wanted to stay with him, she needed to figure out if he was worth giving up a life on the road for. The fact that she thought he just might be scared her half to death.

Now, as she burrowed through the bedding looking for her keys, she found herself wondering what it would be like if she just...stayed. Not in the hotel, but with...him. What would that even look like?

"I can't," Camilla murmured the words as she dug through the wastebasket. "I can't just stay."

As much as she enjoyed the thought of staying with Beau, she couldn't imagine giving up everything she'd worked so hard to accomplish. While he might seem worth it right now, eventually that sort of thing breeds resentment. The last thing she ever wanted to do was to make him hate her, or for her to someday regret giving up the life she had now.

No. If that was the inevitable outcome, she needed to leave now and never look back. Let Beau settle down with Carolyn, who thrived in this atmosphere. Well, maybe not Carolyn. But someone like her, who was meant to be the wife of a rancher.

Wife? Why am I thinking about being a wife?

A handful of dates over a span of days was hardly enough time to be thinking about a future together. No, Camilla needed to get out. Only she still couldn't find her keys. She stood in the center of her room, arms akimbo, and studied the devastation. If she didn't leave soon, she was going to miss her flight.

Finally, she gave up and called the front desk.

"I know this is going to sound crazy. But I can't find the keys to my rental, and I need to get to the airport. Is there anything you can do?"

To her surprise, there was. They could arrange a shuttle to the airport and promised Camilla she wasn't the first guest they'd have to return the rental car. They would look for the keys when they cleaned the room and would take care of returning the car with the agency. In moments, the whole thing had been smoothed over, and Camilla was ready to be on her way.

Only, despite logic and all the thinking she'd done, Camilla didn't want to leave.

"Beau." The name escaped from her in almost a sob. They'd decided last night that it was better to say goodbye at her door when he'd dropped her off. There had been no point in letting things malinger. They'd had a good day and parted as friends. As friends who kissed sometimes. Why spoil it by dragging it out?

A knock at the door drew her back to her senses. The hotel shuttle, no doubt. And here she was woolgathering when she should have been finishing packing. Camilla flung the last couple of things into her suitcase and zipped it up before answering.

"The case is on my bed. I'll be ready to go in a minute," Camilla said as she opened the door, only to find someone other than a hotel representative standing there.

Her eyes went wide. For a moment, Camilla couldn't breathe, afraid that if she did, the illusion would shatter. He wouldn't be there, after all, waiting for her to make the first move. It took a visible amount of effort to pick her jaw up off the floor just so she could utter his name.

"Beau?"

He stood there. His head was down as though he was afraid to look at her as she opened the door. For the longest time, she stood there staring at him, waiting for him to do something, to explain himself and this awful silence. When his head came up, the look in his eyes was an awful thing to see. His gaze was at once sorrowful and tragic, as if he'd lost the only thing that had ever mattered to him.

"This might be the craziest thing I've ever done," he said by way of greeting.

Camilla swallowed hard, trying to get past the lump in her throat. "Should I be nervous?"

He chuckled, and something within her gave way, releasing the tension as he said, "I don't think so."

Camilla started to smile with him, waiting him out. Whatever he was here for, it was going to be okay. Or they would make it okay. "I'm listening."

"Okay, here goes." Beau took a breath, and when he looked at her, his gaze was so intense it scorched her heart. "I'm not asking you to stay."

She nodded. They'd sort of talked about this yesterday. It was at the end of the day while sitting on the front porch of his ranch house, watching the sunset while holding hands. "Okay. That's good, I guess. But then, what are you asking me to do?"

Beau looked away. Camilla watched him struggle to find the words. Her heart broke a little as she watched the muscle work in his jaw and saw how hard this was for him. Finally, after an eternity, Beau lifted his head. When he locked eyes with her this time, it was with a new resolve. "I know you like traveling. That's what you do, right?"

Camilla nodded again. This was true enough.

"I'm asking you if you'd consider traveling more often?"

Camilla was startled. This wasn't what she'd been expecting at all. "How often?"

Beau shoved a hand through his hair, fingers combing through the strands as he thought through his answer; it was slow and deliberate, now, in the things that mattered most. "Well, for starters, if I agree to go see you every other month, will you agree to see me the months in between? I mean...if you're not too busy. If that doesn't work with your schedule, then—"

Her heart burst with joy; Camilla didn't even let him finish. "Yes, I'll do it on one condition."

He stared at her, wide-eyed.

"You have to come see me on my birthday and Christmas."

"Agreed," Beau laughed. The relief was evident on his face and in the way the tension drained out of his shoulders. For the first time since he'd come into the room, he seemed to notice the mess. His gaze fastened on the suitcase still in her hand. "Do you need a ride?"

"Actually...I do." Her gaze went to the mess in the room. "My keys are in here...somewhere. They're supposed to send a shuttle."

"That would be me, I think. Lucy at the front desk called me and said you were having a bit of a crisis."

"Lucy...?"

"We went to high school together."

Camilla shook her head, laughing. "For a city this big, Cheyenne really feels like a small town..."

"Does that mean you don't need the ride?"

"You know something? Why not. You might as well get used to driving me back and forth to the airport."

And just like that, everything clicked into place. It was like taking the perfect picture; when you just knew you had everything lined up exactly where it needed to go in order to create the magic. The next thing she knew, Camilla was laughing. She didn't even realize she was moving until she was in Beau's arms, with her cheek pressed to his chest and her arms so tight around his waist it was doubtful she'd ever let go. Not that he wasn't holding her just as tight as he bent his head to kiss her once, perfectly, exactly in the way she'd been dreaming about for far too long.

The future looked bright.

She couldn't wait to tell Ann.

THE END

Did you enjoy *Focusing on the Cowboy*?

Please consider rating it on Bookbub, Goodreads, or your favorite retailers.

Have you read ***Counting on the Cowboy***?

Join my Newsletter for new releases, sales and other promotions at www.daisylandishromance.com